BEFORE THE
DAWN-WIND
RISES

Laurie B. Clifford

Regal Books

A Division of GL Publications
Ventura, California, U.S.A.

Rights for publishing this book in other languages are contracted by Gospel Literature International foundation (GLINT). GLINT also provides technical help for the adaptation, translation, and publishing of Bible study resources and books in more than 100 languages worldwide. For further information, contact GLINT, Post Office Box 6688, Ventura, California 93006, U.S.A., or the publisher.

Published by Regal Books
A Division of GL Publications
Ventura, California 93006
Printed in U.S.A.

Library of Congress Cataloging in Publication Data

Clifford, Laurie B., 1948-
    Before the dawn-wind rises.

    I. Title.
PS3553.L4377B4   1985   813'54   85-8399
ISBN 0-8307-1049-3

This novel is lovingly dedicated to the One who is
worthy of everything

Before the dawn-wind rises,
before the shadows flee,
I will go to the mountain of myrrh,
to the hill of frankincense.

For me the reward of virtue is to see your face,
and, on waking, to gaze my fill on your likeness.

The Song of Songs 4:6
The Psalms 17:15
(The Jerusalem Bible)

1

We had been married 11 years when I first noticed that Bobby used his fingers to push his food onto his fork. We were having breakfast on the greenhouse porch, autumn blazing like a fandango dancer around us. Janie and Susie were fighting over whose toast had the most cinnamon sugar.

Bobby calmly took both slices, scraped the sugar onto the soil of a potted rubber tree, and handed them back with a fatherly glare. Then he folded his left thumb into his left palm and shoved his scrambled eggs onto his waiting fork with the rest of his fingers.

I looked across the table at him in astonishment. "How long have you been doing that?" I asked, puzzled that I hadn't noticed before.

"Doing what?" He bunched his shaggy blonde eyebrows at me, and shoved another load onto his fork.

"That." I pointed toward his fingers. "How long have you been using your fingers as a pusher?"

"A what?" This time he didn't even look up.

"A *pusher*. Pushing your food onto your fork with your fingers."

Bobby passed me a look that said "space cadet."

"How else do you get all the little pieces on? Missy, don't feed your eggs to Fibber. You know it gives him bad breath."

"You're not supposed to beg, Fibber McGee," Missy scolded, passing on the blame to our blonde Lhasa apso. She followed with a fair imitation of Mrs. Simpson, the Fallstown School principal. "Sweetie, look at me when I'm talking to you."

I studied Bobby in a new light for the rest of the meal, wondering how I could've missed such a major characteristic in someone I'd slept with for 11 years. I guessed I'd been too busy with having babies and trying to find time to take a shower.

"Mommy," Susie yanked on my sleeve. "We're going to be late for school. And I can't find my *souliers*."

"I can't help you," I said blankly. "I don't even know what they are."

"It's French for shoes."

"How do you know that?" I stood up with interest to follow my sleek-haired fourth grader. Another member of my family demonstrating a facet I hadn't noticed. I wondered if she spoke the language fluently. Maybe the whole family jetted over to Paris twice a week while I battled with heel marks on the linoleum.

"Miss Bridges told us. We just learned it yesterday. We're going to learn a new word every day." Susie stood tall and proudly straightened her shoulders. "Today she's going to tell us how to say chair."

"That's a relief."

"What?"

"I mean I'm glad she's teaching you sensible words like *shoe* and *chair*. I mean if she taught you words like *corporate structure* or *fiscal policy*, you wouldn't have much use for them."

Susie opened her closet with a sigh. "See my *souliers* aren't here." She swept her hand across the closet, passing over at least 10 pairs of shoes. Apparently, none of them were *souliers.*

"Are you looking for the ones you wore yesterday?" I asked.

"Mother!" Susie gasped, emphasizing the *ther.* "I can't wear *those.* I wore them *yesterday.*" She put her hands on her hips and sighed again.

"You also wore them in the mud. They're out back waiting for a little elf to wash them off and shine them up."

She threw herself helplessly onto her canopied bed. "Mrs. Simpson says I'll have to clean erasers at recess if I'm late again. Cleaning erasers is yukky." She made a gagging noise.

"Then don't be late," I said. "Stick on a pair of shoes and go for it. You have enough here to shod a tribe of Snoopwiggies."

Susie just moaned. Mentally flipping through the pages of *The Strong-Willed Child* until I located something about letting a child suffer the consequences of her own actions, I fortified myself with expert counsel and walked out, leaving my eldest daughter to her haute couture dilemma.

Long after Janie and Missy had been dispatched out the front door with Fibber McGee as their eager chaperone down the winding country road to the pine schoolhouse, Susie dashed in front of me, kicking up her heels to show me that she'd found her *souliers.*

"Have a good day, honey," I called, wondering as the door slammed how many erasers she'd have to bang and who she'd charm into helping her with the odious task.

All about me, the house fell silent—like an old friend who'd said it all. *How else do you get all the little pieces on the fork?* Bobby's impeccable logic tickled my brain.

Ah my friend, I thought as I wandered out to the greenhouse to clear off the breakfast dishes. *How else? There used to be more than a dozen ways.* I ignored the dishes, sat down in the wicker swinging chair and lifted my face to the streaming sunshine.

One might think I have nothing here to use as a pusher," Miss Burson said in her elegant voice. She cupped her hand and pointed with her pinky across the place setting in front of the class. "One would be gravely mistaken."

Daryl tried to stifle a snort in his throat, but Miss Burson heard it and fixed an icy stare on us. I thought of asking for another freshman etiquette partner. Daryl was always getting us into trouble. Still, he was long and lean and had lips like Elvis.

"As I was saying," Miss Burson continued. "One can always find a pusher if one chooses to look. What could I find here? There is no bread on my plate. Please don't mention my knife. We've already established that a knife is available."

Miss Burson's plate was empty, so I guessed the field was wide open. I raised my hand.

"Yes, Katie Brandon?"

"The celery."

Daryl elbowed me and whispered out the corner of his mouth. "There's no celery, Eyes. The woman is certifiable. Don't let her take you with her."

"Perfect!" Miss Burson clapped her hands in delight. "What else, class?"

Marilyn raised her hand.

"Marilyn DeVry?"

"The carrot stick?" Marilyn tended to be a copy cat.

"Yes. What else?"

Paul raised his hand, and Daryl snickered.

"Paul Steffel?"

"The creamed corn?"

The class burst out laughing.

Miss Burson frowned. "You think it's funny now," she said severely, "but if you were invited to dine at Malacañang Palace tomorrow, Mr. Steffel, you would be summarily evicted. Manners are what divide us from the rest of the animal kingdom. Alas, some of us would rather remain with the classification that is bred on corn mush and sold by the pound."

The class clapped and pelleted Paul with paper wads and pink erasers. Miss Burson went back to her lesson. Daryl drew a pair of mombo lips on my math folder and penciled "the bigger, the better" under them.

"I wouldn't know," I whispered coldly as I erased his artwork.

"You're breaking my heart, Eyes," he whispered. "Tearing it apart."

In the background, a dish clattered to the floor. Fibber had let himself in the pet door, and was greedily scarfing leftovers. "Porker!" I tossed my slipper at him as he dashed back outside, a piece of toast hanging from his mouth.

The telephone rang. "Hang on," I said as I answered it. "I'll get on the cordless." A quick dash through the first floor told me someone had misplaced it again. "I'll call you back," I said, picking up the phone in the study. "Who is this anyway?" I guessed it was Mary Ellen, but it might have been Cammy or Ruth.

"Mrs. Carson?" It was a male voice.

"Who?"

"Mrs. Carson."

"Oh, this is Mrs. Carson. I'm sorry. I thought you were someone else."

"Evidently."

"May I help you?" I borrowed from Miss Burson's proper English. *May requests permission. Can asks if it's possible.*

"I'm calling from the law firm of Atwater and Klein." The voice was cold. It reminded me of my Uncle Clark. "You have been mentioned in Mr. Costain's will. Can you be here at 10 o'clock Monday morning for the reading?"

"What?"

"Mr. Costain's will. D. J. Costain. Monday at 10. The reading." The voice was impatient.

"I don't know any Mr. Costain."

"Well, he must have known you. You are mentioned by name in his will. You are Mrs. Robert Carson, 1012 Oak Tree Lane, Fallstown, California, are you not?"

I hesitated, wondering vaguely if I had amnesia. "Yes, that's me."

"Very well. Ten o'clock?"

"I'll be there."

"Thank you, Mrs. Carson. We'll be looking forward to meeting you."

"Where? Where will you be looking forward to meeting me?" I took down the address of Atwater and Klein. It was in the valley, so I'd have to go down the mountain on Monday morning. Whoever this Mr. Costain was and whatever he'd left me in his will, he'd at least given me an outing all by myself in the city.

The kitchen clock said 9:40. If the house was to be presentable by the time Bobby came home for lunch, the cordless would be essential. As I searched the upstairs, I remembered Missy had used it the evening before.

"Eureka, Admiral Byrd! We found the cordless listening device." It was in Missy's toy box. I dialed Mary Ellen, tucked the phone between my ear and my shoulder, and stripped Missy's bed.

Mary Ellen shrieked when I told her about the will. "Costain? *The* D. J. Costain?" Shriek! Shriek! "You know D. J. Costain and you never told me? Traitor." Shriek! Shriek!

I slipped the cordless down to my hand. "I'm not listening, Mary Ellen," I said into the mouthpiece, "because you're not listening to me. I told you I have no idea who Mr. Costain is.

"Now I'm going to count to five, and when I put my ear back to this phone, I don't want to hear you sounding like a groupie." I waited a moment, counted to five, and pressed the phone back in place.

"Katie, are you there?" Mary Ellen controlled her voice.

"Yes Mary, I'm here."

"D. J. Costain just died."

"Apparently. I gathered that's why they're reading his will."

"He's a famous writer."

"If he's so famous, why haven't I ever heard of him?"

"Because he uses a pen name. Anyway, he writes bodice rippers."

"What?"

"Bodice rippers. You know boy meets girl, boy ravishes girl."

"You're kidding. I thought women wrote those books."

"That's why he used the name Dominique Cardin. No one knew she was a he until he died. It was in this week's *National Enquirer.*" Mary Ellen's voice was deferential. "I have his books, Katie," she said respectfully. "I'll bring them over."

"After lunch," I said. Bobby wasn't going to like this. A mysterious smut writer had designs on his wife. I put down the cordless and dedicated myself to the house, as much to prove to myself as to my husband that I was still a dedicated wife.

2

Bobby called at noon to say he'd be late for lunch. I put the platter of ham sandwiches into the refrigerator and took a packet of orange Jell-O from the cupboard. I'd make it for supper with grated carrots and raisins—yummy, bad for you, and yukky, good for you, in one dish. As I watched the fire bring two cups of water to a full boil, my thoughts returned to my high school years.

They're going to kick Daryl out of school." Marilyn swung around gleefully in her seat to face Carol and me, hunching down to peer at us between the gray bars that outlined the bus seat. "I know why Mr. Donner called him to the office yesterday afternoon. They're going to kick him out of school."

"They don't kick out seniors," Carol said, her voice filled with our mutual disgust for Marilyn and her opinions.

Marilyn singsonged. "They do for some things."

"Not seniors." Carol looked over to reassure me.

"What things?" I demanded, stifling an urge to poke

my fingers through the bars and tweak her nose. It was always in other people's business. But first, I had to find out what Marilyn knew about Daryl Coombs.

"Orgies." Marilyn let the word roll out of her mouth like a hell-fire preacher at a revival meeting. Then she straightened up, nodded her head smugly, and turned around to sit like the good little girl her mother thought she was.

Carol and I just looked at each other and burst out laughing. "How long have you had this fantasy, Mare?" I leaned up and whispered breathlessly into her ear, just loud enough for Carol to enjoy it. "Does Daryl know about it?"

Marilyn's ear turned colors, but she didn't satisfy me by defending herself. *She knows I'll rip her to shreds,* I thought dramatically as I slouched back in my seat. *The little weasel.*

The bus lurched to a stop in front of Eddie Brighton's house, and the wind blew in the rain as Eddie scrambled aboard. "Howie's sick," he notified Armando, the bus driver, as he swept past. That meant no more stops before school. Armando adjusted his cap, swung the bus down a side street, and slid it into the great race of Manilan traffic.

The rain, as if sensing it had less than an hour to wrestle us off the road, picked up intensity, and hurled its cacophony against the metal shell around us. From my protected vantage, I watched pedestrians slosh down Rizal Boulevard. It was the same city that had greeted me almost four years before.

My first impression of Manila was one of mud. Not ordinary puddles here and there, but an ocean of mud stretching from the airplane door as far as I could see. My father was there to welcome us, standing at the bottom of the stairs, boots to his knees and raincoat to his ankles. Under his arms, I counted five umbrellas.

"Mabuhay! Welcome to Manila," he greeted us in his hearty voice. "They call this maputik." He gestured enthusiastically at the mud. *I call it mud,* I thought, painfully aware of the breathtaking Vermont autumn I would be missing. Then, reminding myself of my vow to be a good sport, I picked up my little sister, Meg, and ran for it.

It was impossible to deplane in a thunder shower, greet our father whom we hadn't seen in two months, and get under an umbrella fast enough to keep from being soaked. If the welcoming committee at the parsonage had mistaken us for refugees, I wouldn't have faulted them.

I spent the next two weeks exploring our new home, tramping barefoot and bareheaded in the constant downpour of typhoon season. The warm rain and wild winds courted my favor like a persistent lover. Before the rains stopped, I was in love with the typhoons.

Then another suitor came to call. Dazzling blue and green. Sky, ocean, and countryside. Manila sparkled in the hot sun. In the weeks to come, I fell in love with Manila as I saw it from the back of my father's Lambretta motor scooter.

Traffic was jammed everywhere in Manila. My father sized up the situation, and concluded a motor scooter was the answer. We called it Gertrude. He drove Gerty without mercy, and with only one problem. His family was one too many. Either his wife or his oldest daughter had to find another means of transportation when the whole family went out together.

Still, my father's ingenuity in assembling the rest of the family like a jigsaw on his motor scooter was commendable. He would sit on the driver's seat with my mother or me on the passenger's seat behind him. Karl would sit between us on a pillow. Meg would perch on the bit of seat that protruded between my father's legs. And John would stand in front of Meg, bravely parting the wind for the rest of us.

The school bus ground to a halt at the bottom of Hope Hill, ending my reverie. "Hang on," Armando warned us as he shifted into reverse. We were going to make a run for it. *I'll bet we walk up again,* I thought pessimistically. It would be the second time that week.

The faded blue bus rushed the steep hill, grabbed the road, crawled halfway up, shuddered, and died. Armando stuck two fingers into his mouth and whistled. "Everybody out. This is as far as she goes, folks."

Marilyn ducked behind Carol and me, using our bodies for shelter as we climbed the hill. "Inhale, exhale, inhale, exhale." She pretended to be supervising gymnastics. "Inhale, expell, inhale, expell, expell, expell, expell . . . "

I turned around calmly, twirling my umbrella so the water flipped in her face. "I'm so sorry about your illness, Mare," I gushed. "It's too bad personality transplants aren't more advanced."

Who's D. J. Costain?" Bobby scraped his feet on the mat, bellowing the question from the front door. I kept stirring the Jell-O, waiting for him to come into the kitchen. "Who is D. J. Costain?" he repeated, standing next to the bar, his burly figure blocking the passageway into the dining room. It was his I'll-defend-what's-mine posture.

"Who told you about D. J. Costain?" I demanded.

Bobby hesitated, not sure if he was still the injured party. "Sam Gless told me on my way down here." He cleared his throat.

"Sam Gless? Sam Gless?" My voice rose. "How did Sam Gless of all people find out?"

"He was down at Wharton's helping Joel fix Margie's washer when she got a phone call." Bobby came toward me, a conciliatory slope to his shoulders.

I backed away. "I didn't call Margie." I'd called Cammy and Ruth, and then spent the rest of the morning on the phone with Mary Ellen.

"Arlene was over at Cindy's using her microwave when Karen dropped by. Karen was over at Cammy's when you called. Arlene called Margie."

"Just a minute. Let me get this straight." I boosted myself up onto the kitchen counter, displacing my anger with fascination over Fallstown's 60 minute grapevine, more reliable than any communication device yet invented by man. You could trust the grapevine to whisk any secret to the ears of the person you most wanted to keep it from in 60 minutes or your money back.

"I called Cammy. Karen happened to be there. Karen dropped by Cindy's. Arlene happened to be there. Arlene called Margie. Sam Gless happened to be there. Sam told you."

"Right. Now who is D. J. Costain?"

"This is why I'm losing all my marbles up here." I was angry again. "This is a textbook example." I shook my finger at him. "Don't you argue with me, Robert Carson!"

Bobby pursed his lips. "Truce." He made a time out sign with his hands. "I'll go outside and come in again." Then he tramped back through the living room, closed the front door, waited a moment, and swung it open again. "Hi, honey, I'm home. Boy, that smells good! Whatever it is, I hope it's for lunch."

I looked hurriedly about the kitchen for something that might be sending out an odor. Beside me was a can of cat food. "It's tuna and liver," I called back, reading the label. "You'll probably be happier with the ham sandwiches in the fridge."

Bobby came up behind me and put his arms around my waist, snuggling down into my neck. "Friends?" he whispered.

"Friends," I said.

That's what's wrong with you, Bobby Jay, I thought as I carried the plate of sandwiches out onto the porch. *You're so irresistible. I've never been able to resist you. Not since the first time we met on the beach at Santa Barbara. And so here I am in Fallstown. Where would I be if you weren't so irresistible?*

By the time we kissed good-bye under the shedding oak tree in the front yard, I had succeeded in convincing Bobby that I really didn't know a D. J. Costain, and that whoever he was, he was no threat to our marriage.

Collecting threats to our marriage was one of Bobby's favorite pastimes. I thought he did it more for the fun of having me placate him—like a mother reassuring her child that the boogie man was nowhere around—than because he really feared for our relationship.

"What time are we supposed to be there on Monday?" He stopped at the end of our driveway, and called back to me.

"Ten o'clock," I yelled. Then he waved, and I waved back.

Ten o'clock. I'm supposed to be there at 10 o'clock, I thought as I watched him jog down the lane. *You'll just have to give me back my wings for a few hours this time, Bobby Jay.* I didn't know exactly why, but I knew I was going to Atwater and Klein alone on Monday morning.

3

I t's only *Wednesday!* How can you stand to wait? I'm
going to die of suspense before Monday." Mary Ellen
puffed for breath under the oak tree, a large box of
books at her feet. "How come they can't read the will to
you tomorrow instead? It's cruel to make you wait so
long."

"Probably standard procedure. Makes somebody
feel important. Anyway, the man who called wasn't
exactly chatty. How many books did the article say he
wrote?"

"Sixty-one romances as Dominique Cardin, 13 how-
to books as D. J. Carrington, and 23 mystery-adventures
as D. J. Carpenter."

"And nobody ever saw him? No pictures? No
interviews? A complete mystery man." I shook my head
and followed Mary Ellen inside. Then I knelt on the
living room rug and emptied the box.

Romances were Mary Ellen's not-so-secret vice. She
had shelves of them in her basement. Fifty-four of D. J.
Costain's 61 soon covered the floor in front of me.

"Are they any good?" I picked up a paperback with
a melon-breasted woman on the cover. "I mean

compared to other romances, are they any good?"

"The best." Mary Ellen searched for a particular title. "Listen to this one." She picked up a book called "The Flaming Circle," flipped to the middle, and began to read. "Rachel knew—"

"Just a minute," I interrupted. "I have to get comfortable." I leaned against the couch, tucked my feet under my legs, closed my eyes, and tried to erase the prejudice I'd already built up against the book merely from it's cover. "OK, go."

Mary Ellen began again, her voice low and sensuous. "Rachel knew Travis had mastered her heart just as he had mastered her body that stormy night so long ago. She knew she remained his prisoner. The door to her heart, locked after that brief encounter, could only be opened by his key."

Mary Ellen paused. "If only the passion in her heart, the undying ember that had smoldered unseen for so many years, could warm the fragile body that lay silently on the hospital bed beside her. 'Have I come too late, my darling?' Rachel whispered earnestly as she pressed his pale hand to her pounding heart."

I blushed unnoticed as Rachel reacquainted the unconscious Travis with her apparently wrinkle-free body. When Mary Ellen finished reading, I tried to camouflage my uneasiness with humor. "They ought to call it *The Flaming Melons*," I said, risking a look in her direction, but she was staring off into space, swept away by D. J. Costain's torrid prose.

I pressed my tongue between my teeth, suppressing a strong desire to activate a longstanding debate over Mary Ellen's "harmless" reading material. Picking up another Costain paperback entitled, *Love's Carousel,* I began to read, hoping to find something I could like.

Miss Burson has dirty books under her bed." Carol whispered into my ear as we found places in our world religions class.

I whispered back. "How do you know?"

"I saw them. In a box under her bed."

"Class!" Miss Burson brought the class to order with a decisive clap. "This week we're discussing the origins of Buddhism."

Carol drew a picture of a corpulent Buddha reading a book. Underneath she captioned, "Buddha borrows one of Flossie's dirty books."

Flossenthia Burson was a spinster in her early forties. She had taught at Hope Academy since the school's beginnings as a response to the growing American community in the Philippine Islands. In the evenings and on weekends, she supplied creative tension for female boarding students by serving as their housemother.

Miss Burson was easily the most loved and the most hated teacher in school. No one was indifferent to her. I loved her. I'd never met anyone like her. Like Mary Poppins, she was unique. The world didn't define Flossie Burson, Flossie Burson defined the world.

Now, in my junior world religions class, I studied my teacher carefully, a new aspect to her character emerging in my mind. What kind of dirty books did she keep under her bed? I had to know.

Taking my notebook and setting it on my lap, I wrote slowly, hoping Miss Burson wouldn't notice my arm movements. "What kind of dirty books?"

Carol eased her hand over to write. "Ripping, tearing ones. I'll show you after lunch."

The rest of the class period, I devoted my devious genius to the problem of Miss Burson's bed chamber.

Dormitories were off limits for all students during school hours. And houseparents' rooms were sacrosanct at all times.

I had three friends whom I trusted with my life: Carol Shavers, Mayda Martel, and Daryl Coombs. Carol, Mayda, and I had been best friends since ninth grade. Our families were all new in Manila, giving us a common history.

Strangely, however, Daryl, with whom I had neither gender nor experience in common, had been a best friend since the ninth grade as well. Daryl was an enigma at Hope Academy. He had been a boarding student since the first grade, but he had never fit in. There were whispered rumors that he came from a "difficult home." That his parents weren't "happy" or "orthodox," as if the two were one and the same.

He was the kind of kid who "served as a bad influence," "wasted his potential," "mocked authority," and generally "caused trouble." In my opinion, Daryl was simply the kind of kid who should have been spared childhood. And regardless of his rebellious nature, he had been my faithful friend since we bumped into each other the first day of school, spilling our new books down the stairs.

The older girls' boarding house was a white two-story building, next to the long Quonset hut that served as a combination chapel/cafeteria. Miss Burson's room was on the first floor, guarding the stairs. With Daryl stationed in front to whistle a warning, and Mayda parked in back to help us through Miss Burson's window, Carol and I could safely sneak into her room right after lunch.

"Dirty books?" Daryl's eyes shone at the thought when I told him my plan. "How many?"

We were on our way to the cafeteria. "Carol!" I motioned for her and Mayda to catch up. "How many dirty books?" I whispered.

"A bunch."

"More than 25?" Daryl asked, as if the number had special significance.

Carol nodded.

"Then you have to bring me one, Eyes."

"That's stealing," Mayda said severely.

Daryl activated his Elvis lip. "It's borrowing. She has so many, she won't notice it's gone. I just want to see how dirty it is. Then we'll put it back." I could tell Mayda wanted to see a book too, because she didn't object.

After the noontime blessing, we nibbled a few obligatory bites of our tuna sandwiches, stirred our mixed vegetables around on our plates, and faded out a side door. Daryl lolled in front of the girls' dorm, a favorite activity anyway because he thought it was interpreted as a threat to their virginity.

Mayda, Carol, and I ambled to the back of the older girls' dorm, remarked on the weather for a moment, then unhooked the large screen that protected Flossie's pink and white boudoir from flying insects and other annoyances. Miss Burson's canopied bed was every little girl's delight. Tea in her room, selectively bestowed on the smaller girls not in her charge but definitely under her spell, was a thing of wonder, to be proudly whispered about after lights out.

Although I had been to her room before, I stood in the middle of it now marveling at its femininity until Carol pulled my hand, urging me toward the bed. Kneeling down and reaching under the bed with one motion, we pulled out a coat box, slid off the lid, and stared inside.

I barely had time to glance over its contents before Mayda hissed at the window. "Daryl just whistled! Get out of there!"

I hesitated, not knowing which book to take. The covers were all pretty much the same—wind-swept women staring down toward the sea, riding on horseback, or gazing up at Victorian mansions. I grabbed the closest one, and Carol slid the top back on the box.

The door to Miss Burson's room opened just as we hooked back the window screen and ducked our heads below it. "I won't have you calling any of my children bad, Prue," she was saying to the little girls' housemother. "It's a categorical word, and it's not fit for children."

"He's not one of your children," Miss Kraemer replied.

"They're all my children," Miss Burson said tersely.

It was time to move on. Realizing I had nowhere to hide the book, I stashed it in my underpants and followed my friends, hoping no one would notice my awkward gait.

The warning bell rang as we reached the class buildings, leaving no time for a group conference around the illicit book. Since none of us had the right to examine it without the others, I went to the girls' restroom, fished it out of my underpants and dropped it into the trash barrel to be rescued after school.

Daryl grabbed me in the hall after our last class of the day. "Get it." He lowered his eyelids and adjusted his top lip. "Meet me over by the gym." There was a basketball game at four o'clock so we had an hour to spare.

Nobody noticed us as we congregated under the bleachers and skimmed over the paperback for the dirty parts. In the background, balls bounced and belled pompoms rattled as the varsity players and cheerleaders warmed up.

"This isn't dirty at all. It's just like Grace Livingston

Hill, and *everyone* reads those," Carol said when a meticulous second search failed to yield anything naughty.

"The paperback covers fooled you, Carol," Daryl said with unexpected sympathy. I had anticipated a sarcastic remark, underscored by a lecture on the ways of the world.

"It's OK," I said. "I'm glad Miss Burson isn't really reading dirty books. Let's get this back before she misses it."

On the way to the girls' dorm, I tugged on Daryl's arm and pulled him back from the others. "Thanks for saving Carol's feelings," I said.

"Nothin' to it, Eyes. Never have been one to hurt a lady." He hurled his jackknife into the air in a face-saving gesture designed to mask the fact that he cared.

4

C all them." Mary Ellen woke from her reverie and urged me to change my appointment with Atwater and Klein.

"What'll I tell them?"

"Just say tomorrow or Friday is more convenient for you than Monday. Tell them you live up in the mountains and your car will be in the garage for repairs on Monday."

"That's not true."

"Yes, it is. I'm going to break it this weekend." She gestured impatiently. "Just *call* them!"

Mary Ellen was used to having her way. Since there were no children, her husband, Bud, catered to her as if she were an only child. I didn't mind standing up to her if necessary. It helped keep me in shape for Susie. But I wanted to find out what was in D. J. Costain's will as much as she did.

"Here goes." I walked to the kitchen with Mary Ellen behind me like a shadow at midday, got the number of Atwater and Klein from the operator, and dialed.

"Law offices of Atwater and Klein. May I help you?"

The voice was young and sweet.

"Yes. This is Mrs. Carson." I twisted my hair nervously. "Someone—a gentleman—called me this morning about the reading of Mr. Costain's will on Monday?"

"Yes?"

Mary Ellen and I had conjectured that this reading of D. J. Costain's will was exclusively for me since according to the *National Enquirer,* he had lived in New England. But now I wondered if we were wrong. "Will there be anyone else there?" My voice cracked in the middle of anyone.

"Just a moment. I'll check." The secretary switched the telephone to Muzak.

"Well?" Mary Ellen crowded her ear next to mine. I had been silent a second too long.

"'Moon River?'" I let her have the phone.

"What?"

"They're playing 'Moon River.' The secretary went to check with somebody."

"She's back!" Mary Ellen handed me the receiver like a hot potato.

"Mrs. Carson?"

"Yes."

"It was Mr. Klein who called you. But your appointment on Monday is with Mr. Atwater. Mr. Klein is in court next week."

"Just me and Mr. Atwater?"

"I can sit in if you're nervous," she suggested.

"Oh no, that's not what I meant. It's just that I'm hoping to change the day if there's no one else involved." I chose my words carefully, fighting back the desire to pour out my bewilderment and plead with her to enlighten me.

"Just a moment." Pages rustled in the background. "So far, any Monday would be fine," she said.

"Oh no. I don't want to delay it. I was hoping to move it up. You see, I've never met Mr. Costain—not to my knowledge anyway—and I'm understandably curious as to why he would mention me in his will."

Mary Ellen nudged me furiously. "Tell her the truth. You're *dying*!"

The secretary laughed a musical little sound I associated with secretaries. "I see," she said. "But I'm afraid it's impossible. The will specifically says you are to be notified on a Wednesday, and the will is to be read to you on a Monday."

"Thank you very mu-much," I stuttered.

Mary Ellen sat there making Twilight Zone noises when I told her that our present suspense had been provided intentionally by Mr. Costain. "Have you read any of his mystery-adventure novels?" I asked.

She shook her head. "But this definitely could be the plot for one. Somebody's toying with your emotions, child."

"Maybe it's a hoax." I picked up the receiver and dialed the Better Business Bureau in the valley.

"If it's a hoax, the perpetrator is D. J. Costain himself," I told Mary Ellen when I hung up, "because Atwater and Klein is A-1 respectable."

When my three daughters bounced in from school at 2:30, Mary Ellen and I were still in the kitchen. She was hatching an elaborate plot to kidnap the sweet-voiced secretary and hold her hostage for a copy of the will. I shoved a cookie in her mouth to shush her.

"Welcome home, sweeties." I kissed their foreheads, hoping to sense whether news of my morning had reached them through the grapevine. Nothing. "Snack's ready." I motioned toward the milk and cookies on the bar. "How was school?"

"Howie Jenkins wiped cooties on me," Missy complained.

After we had discussed cooties, Sarah Jenkins' underwear, cumulus clouds, and warts, I told them my news. "I got an interesting phone call this morning. I have to go down to the valley on Monday." I tried to make it sound as boring and matter-of-fact as possible.

"I know you're happy about this, Mommy," Janie said philosophically, after I'd convinced them D. J. Costain wasn't a movie star and wasn't leaving me a million dollars. "You'll have something new to tell Daddy when he gets home."

I didn't enlighten her. They returned to cooties. Were cooties germs or were they worse? Later, after they were in bed, "Daddy" coaxed me down memory lane. "Come on. Think back. Maybe it's somebody you knew way, way back."

Upstairs in our big four poster bed, I didn't want to remember anymore. I'd been over and over my past, from my first memory of my father pushing me in my stroller to all the newest ones, most of which revolved around D. J. Costain, a man I was certain I didn't know.

"Obviously, he was an eccentric person, Bobby," I said, restraining my impatience. "He probably saw me somewhere, thought I looked like the heroine of one of his books, and willed me an autographed copy."

We were on our backs looking up at the knotty pine ceiling. Bobby rolled over and studied me carefully. "I wouldn't blame him if he took you for a dream come true," he said tenderly, tracing my features with his index finger. "You are beautiful, Katie Carson."

"I'm not fishing." I contemplated a particularly dark knot on the ceiling. "I'm only saying that however D. J. Costain thought he knew me, it was something quirky like that."

"I mean it. You're beautiful." His lips hovered above mine.

We made love, more aware of each other than we

had been the night before, as if a stranger's sudden intrusion into our lives had reminded us that our love was not inevitable. Each of us could have chosen someone else, yet even 11 years of marriage didn't make the choosing less immediate.

Afterwards, as I lay in Bobby's arms, I thought of his first words to me. "I've always wondered where the sunset came from. Now I know it comes from your eyes." I had looked up to see a stocky man in a blue bathing suit. He reminded me of my favorite childhood teddy bear.

I frowned. "What?" The words were disjointed and didn't make sense to me.

The teddy bear man tried again, this time succeeding with the transition, but still sounding as if he was reciting for a school play. "I've always wondered where the sunset came from. Now I know it comes from your eyes."

"Who told you to say that?"

"Killer says it works every time."

"Who's Killer?"

"Lady Killer Kaberski back on campus, UCSB."

"It's ridiculous. It doesn't make sense."

"You're talking to me, aren't you?"

"Yes. I guess I am."

"Well, then it works. It doesn't matter if it makes sense." Mr. Bear sat down beside me, leaving a reassuring slice of sand between us, and held out his hand. "I'm Bobby Carson, senior in business at UCSB."

I shook it. "I'm Katie Brandon, sophomore in confusion at Westmont College."

"Aha." He nodded. "I remember that one." He slit his eyes and tried a Chinese accent. "Confusion say light at end of tunnel only lead to more confusion."

I stared at him, delighted. No one had ever phrased it so succinctly for me. "But you're not majoring in confusion anymore?"

"Nope. I found out life's like football. Sometimes you just have to drop back and punt. I was running around trying to keep up with the 'in' crowd, be Mr. Cool, and all that garbage. Then I realized nobody cared, so I decided to drop back and just be myself."

"And it was that easy to find out who 'myself' was?" He seemed so confident, I was sure what his answer would be.

"I've always known," he said with a smile. "I just spent a couple of years trying to hide it from my peers on campus. I guess I assumed that when I went away to college, I'd become Robert J. Carson, suave, sophisticated businessman. When I found I was still Bobby Jay, original country boy, I thought I should at least hide it."

He lifted his head and roared. "As if I could! Look at me? Do I look like a city slicker?"

"You have a bathing suit on," I reminded him. "It's hard to tell right now."

"Well, my manners," he insisted. "Do I have city manners? I mean I couldn't even make a little come-on line believable."

"I see your point. So where are you from?" Bobby Jay was picking me up, right there on the beach, but I didn't care. It had been a friendless two years, and I didn't care.

"It's a little town up in the San Bernardino mountains. Post office, school house, community church, combination cafe/general store/gas station, real estate office, and about 700 homes, most of which aren't year round. It's called Fallstown because it sits at the bottom of a 60-foot waterfall."

Bobby shone all over. "My dad owns the real estate company. Has branches in the valley and up in Big Bear. Both my brothers and both my brothers-in-law work with him. I'm going to take over the Fallstown office when I graduate." He ran his hands over his hairy arms as he spoke.

The world Bobby described as we sat watching the sun go down was the most secure, cohesive world I could imagine. From the time this youngest Carson joined it, he found love and fullness waiting for him, as if God purposed to make it up to one little boy for all the other little boys who went to bed hungry.

"It's beautiful," I said when he finished talking. "Like something out of a fairy tale, only without witches or goblins."

"Exactly." He turned to me eagerly. "I want to show it to you." My new teddy bear friend quivered with good will. "I know you'll see it just the way I do."

Now Bobby's gentle snoring told me I could sneak out of his arms. Gretchen, the Whartons' Saint Bernard, woofed at the moon in the forest behind us. *She's out again,* I thought. *Margie'll be running after her any minute.* Margie's husband, Joel, wouldn't wake up for death.

Envying the excuse for a midnight stroll, I slid out of bed and into my lambskin slippers. *Maybe I'll get her before Margie does,* I decided, allowing myself the rationale I was seeking.

"Gretchen," I called softly, the night air crisp against my cheeks. "Here girl." I whistled into the soft breeze that played harmonies in the towering pines. "Gretchen."

"I got her, Katie." Margie hauled Gretchen from the forest on my right. "Did she wake you up?"

"No. I just wanted an excuse for a walk."

"Good night, Kate."

"Good night, Margie."

I know you'll see it just the way I do, Katie. Bobby's voice seemed to come to me on the breeze. "I try Bobby Jay," I whispered. "Honey, I try."

5

Thursday morning, I woke with the first light, dressed in a hurry, and went to visit my own bit of heaven. Oak Tree Lane dead-ended into the San Bernardino National Forest which cradled our home on two sides with peace and solitude. I often thought that I wouldn't have survived 11 years in Fallstown if this weren't so, if I had been surrounded by neighbors to monitor my life.

Here in the forest, I left all my roles behind. I didn't have to be anybody's anything—wife, mother, daughter-in-law, best friend. Here in the forest, especially in the early morning, I could just be. I scrambled over a small ravine and up an incline to a fallen tree.

Hopping up near the roots, I held my arms out for balance and tiptoed along the trunk, a song fragment from girlhood tumbling into my mind. "Four little monkeys up in the tree . . . "

I began to whistle, then to sing. "One fell down and then there were three . . . " The early morning world around me sang along. "Hey, stop your counting! That's not a monkey, that's just me."

I reached the decaying branches and straddled them victoriously as if I had just felled the tree with my own hands. There was something heady about this morning, some quality that set it apart from the ones that preceded it.

It was the will. As chagrined as I was to admit that D. J. Costain, "sleaze writer" in Bobby's words, had added something to my life, it was true. Now—alone with the events of yesterday—I began to understand why I felt so freed by such a ridiculous incident.

It was the unmerited favor of it. I had been summoned to the reading of Mr. Costain's will for no reason I knew of. I had done nothing to elicit it, nothing to deserve it, nothing to win it. There was absolutely no performance attached to it. I didn't have to be anything or do anything for it. I only had to show up.

Class, I have one assignment for you over Easter vacation." Mr. Stigwell adjusted his glasses, ignoring our cries of protest. "Your bodies will be on vacation, but your minds don't have to be on hold. Anyway, it's very simple. Write a two-page essay—more if you like—on the following question. This is a subjective essay. Use personal experience." He chalked it on the board. "What Is a Friend?"

After school, Mayda shook her raven hair and popped her gum. "How am I going to write two pages on that?"

"I know how I'm going to write it." Paul brushed up against her, knocking her books to the floor, and spying into her cleavage as she bent to pick them up. "A friend is fabulous to look at . . . "

"A friend is somebody who doesn't take advantage of friends," I said sharply. "He did that on purpose, May. Make him pick them up."

"I did not. But as a gentleman and a scholar, I'll be happy to help the lady." Paul knelt down to look in Mayda's eyes as if it were a late night tête-à-tête.

Mayda blushed, thanked him sweetly, and followed me to the bus. *A friend is someone who still likes you even though you act stupid,* I thought, contemplating my voluptuous friend who refused to recognize that boys had "bad things" on their minds. *How can she be 15 years old and be so naive?*

"I'm going to write that essay Gertrude Stein style," Howie crowed as Armando idled the engine. Standing in the aisle, he bowed to his captive audience and cleared his throat. "Ladies and Gentlemen, a friend is a friend is a friend is a friend . . . "

Someone threw a paper wad at him.

At home, I found my mother in her bedroom studying Albanian. She adopted obscure languages like Carol's mother adopted stray cats. "We're supposed to write a two-page essay for English," I informed her.

"On what?" She put her book down on the lamp table and patted the bedside.

"What Is a Friend?" I sat down beside her, absorbing the love she cast over me.

"That won't be hard." She smiled.

"All my life, my favorite memory will be coming home to you after school." I reached over to give her a warm hug.

She smiled again, and I knew I had pleased her.

"I'm going to write it now. Get it over with so I won't have to think about it."

My mother nodded her approval.

After pineapple juice and crackers, Meg, who didn't go to school because there wasn't a kindergarten, joined me at my desk. I wrote her name on a blank sheet of paper, and told her, "You'll have to practice your name quietly Meggie because Katie has to think."

Meg wrinkled her brow to show me she understood thinking.

Then I chewed on my pencil, and thought of the friends I'd known. About why some of them had lasted while others had drifted away. A tropical breeze lifted the curtains, and the sounds of Manila's street life wafted up to me, comforting and familiar.

By the time I began to write, Meg had tired of her labors and had run down to join my brothers in the yard. "Most of all, a friend doesn't ask you to change. A friend accepts you just like you are. True friendship is a decision, not an emotional response. I choose my friends carefully because I don't believe it's right to unchoose them when they don't please me."

I glanced at my wristwatch. It was past time to be starting breakfast. Breathing deeply, I took in the morning and the solitude, let them settle down inside me, and headed for home, refreshed and renewed.

Janie was waiting for me in the kitchen. She had taken the juice out of the freezer and was struggling with the wrapper. "Thanks for starting breakfast," I said softly, my eyes caressing my middle child.

What makes her so sensitive to others, and how much will she suffer because of it? I wondered as we worked side by side. Three daughters in three years. One, two, three little darlings all in row. How was it that each was so different from the others?

With Susie, I assumed the precious little thing that nuzzled my breast was mine to shape and mold. With Janie, I suspected genetic interference. By the time Missy came, I realized the best I could do was to discover who my daughters were born to be and applaud.

In my years of mothering, I had learned to relax.

Instead of assuming responsibility to *make* them, now I
knew I was responsible only to guide them. The
difference allowed me laughing places.

After breakfast, I walked the girls to school, with
Susie and a group of friends running ahead and Fibber
barking jealously at my heels. "Forgive me for stealing
your moment of glory," I told him playfully, "but I'm
jogging from the school house to the post office and you
may come with me."

I had his chain in my windbreaker. When we
reached the school, I snapped it onto his collar, blew
kisses to my daughters, and took off. The half-mile jog
down to the post office was a monument to self-
deception. Jogging down the road, I convinced myself
the American woman could have it all. Dragging back
up, I made Erma Bombeck my patron saint.

Two envelopes with familiar handwriting were
waiting for me in our mailbox. The first was a fat
brown envelope from my mother, the second, a small
white one from Carol Shavers.

I opened the first one immediately, sitting on the
curb beside the post office to read the comings and
goings of my beloved faraway family. Mother always
began her letters by identifying the physical location of
each family member.

"Meg is in the kitchen cooking dinner. Your father is
talking to Ernesto Jose, our new deacon, on the phone.
Karl and Lita are downstairs with little John. Big John
. . . " I read to the end without stopping, and then read
it through again, slowly.

When we left Vermont for Manila, it was to be a
short-term assignment filling in for Pastor Stringham.
But when Pastor Stringham died, my parents stayed on,
and the Philippine Islands became home. Now they
only came back to the United States for short,
obligatory visits.

Karl had graduated from the University of the Philippines, married a Filipina, and settled down in the first floor apartment of my parent's home to raise a family. John and Meg were both students at the university and had no desire to move back. It seemed the only thing my family truly missed about the United States of America was me, my husband, and our three daughters.

I had been over and over it in my mind: how I alone came to be separated from the Brandon clan. *My parents chose life in the Philippines. It was an adult choice for them,* I would tell myself. *Karl, John, and Meg were practically born there. It's natural for them to want to stay. I was the only one who had been caught between cultures. The first 13 years in Vermont. Those important teenage years in Manila.*

I fingered the letter from Carol; the postmark said Haiti. I never knew where she'd write from. *I'll save you for later,* I decided. Pocketing the letters, I began the chug uphill. Carol had been caught between cultures too. All three of us, Carol, Mayda, and I, had been sliced from one life and spliced into another, moving to Manila in the summer of our thirteenth year. When school began, we gradually blossomed into old timers at Hope Academy.

Perched on a hilltop overlooking Manila, Hope presided over the best and the worst years of our lives. Love and hate mixed and mingled to form cords that tied us forever, but didn't make us want to go back. Growing up wasn't easy, and the place that marshalled our days, took on forever all the unruly emotions of those tangled up years.

It seemed to me as I walked, however, that my friends had resolved the dichotomy of their upbringing better than I had.

6

When I puffed into the log cabin offices of Carson and Sons, Bobby was behind his desk, chair tipped back, boots on the desktop, barking into a white telephone receiver that looked like a child's toy in his big hand. I sat down on the Naugahyde couch to catch my breath.

"Yes sir, that's right." He was talking to a client. "There's a federal moratorium on building up here." He "smoked" his pencil and punctuated the air with it as he talked, reminding me of a Jerry Lewis movie we had watched on our honeymoon. "The beaches are full. The mountains are the only place to get away anymore. Real estate up here can only do one thing—appreciate!"

I tried unsuccessfully not to laugh. Across the street, Amy McPherson filled her new station wagon with unleaded. I knocked on the window and waved to her.

"Mom's over at Karen's," Bobby said as he hung up. "What do you think of the Sheridan place?" He pointed to a new photograph in the center of the *For Sale* display. Bobby knew all the buildings in Fallstown like old friends, and referred to each by the name of the original owner.

"It looks nice. I'd buy it for $110,000," I said. "All that paint paid off. I'll go by and see your mother. I'm sure Karen's told her about the will by now."

Bobby raised his eyebrows, puckered up for a kiss, and dialed a new number. Obediently, I puckered back, combed his unruly hair with my fingers, and waved good-bye. "Come on, lazybones." I tugged on Fibber's leash to get him started back up the hill.

As I walked, I rehearsed answers to questions Mother Carson might ask about D. J. Costain and his will. Bobby's mother and father had always been kind and considerate toward me. At times I thought they were too solicitous, as if my background made them nervous. But it would have been in bad taste for them to show it, like insulting a clergyman.

They referred to my parents' "work" in generous terms, using a tone they reserved for funerals and catastrophic events. I sometimes suspected Bobby's mother of being afraid I would whisk him away to some far corner of the globe.

Karen ran to the front door to greet me. "It's so exciting about the will," she whispered, nodding toward the kitchen. Apparently D. J. Costain's will was already on Mother Carson's let's-not-discuss-it list. But Karen's eyes sparkled with tell-me-everything wonder. I hugged her and we went into the kitchen arm-in-arm.

Martin and Susannah Carson had raised two daughters sandwiched between three sons. It was a hearty western family whose only lasting sorrow was the loss of a third daughter, Julie, born prematurely two years after Bobby. They guarded their offspring like jewels in a sovereign's crown, welcoming their children's mates as accessories to set off each jewel's brilliance.

I loved Karen, Bobby's closest sibling. In her Scandinavian beauty, she resembled her mother, but it was in her eagerness to experience life beyond the San Bernardino mountains that our souls met.

Mother Carson was standing over the turn-of-the-century stove Kevin had refitted for gas. Behind her, the sun shone through gingham curtains, highlighting her satiny skin. "I'm sure there's a simple explanation, dear," she said, tight-lipped and firm as if speaking to a teenager caught out past curfew.

I tried to answer, but she seemed afraid to listen. "I'm fixing your favorite, split pea soup and cornbread for lunch. I just talked to Bobby. He's coming up at noon." Her voice softened as she spoke of her baby. "We'll just relax and enjoy each other as if we have nothing better to do."

She turned to smile at me now, and I melted as I always did. "There isn't anything better to do, is there?" I said to please her, crossing the room to hug her aproned figure. She was irresistible. Just like her son.

The three of us sat in the kitchen, making fruit salad and passing around family gossip until Bobby arrived for lunch. Mother and Father Carson had homes in Fallstown, Big Bear, and Yucaipa, distributing their time between Bobby and Karen, Marty in Big Bear, and Tommy and Alice in the valley. Presently, their clan numbered 32 in all.

Mother Carson waited until Bobby said grace and dipped his spoon into the steaming split peas. "Ivy's thinking of taking the kids back east for Thanksgiving this year." She used her national disaster voice.

Bobby didn't seem to notice. "She hasn't been back to see her parents in awhile," he said between mouthfuls.

"Robert." His mother's voice jerked his spoon to a halt in midair. "We've *always* been together on Thanksgiving."

"I'm sorry, Mom." Bobby's voice was tender. "I

wasn't thinking." Julie had lived for one day,
Thanksgiving Day, 30 years before. He tossed me a
pleading expression that didn't need words. Ivy was an
in-law. Carson ethics dictated that another in-law
should talk to her first, avoiding direct confrontation
with a blood family member if possible.

"I'll talk to her, Mom," I said quietly, knowing that
by doing so I would offset any demerits D. J. Costain
had caused me. Mother Carson beamed her what-more-
could-a-mother-in-law-ask-for approval.

I called Ivy as soon as I reached home, more to get
it over with than to intrude on her personal life. I
admired Ivy. Of all the in-laws, she had the most grit.
Still, I felt she had some things to learn about
compromise.

"Mom told you?" Guessing the reason for my call,
Ivy skipped the usual preliminaries.

"Ivy!"

"Just give it to me, Kate. Let's not arf around as if
you're not calling about Thanksgiving."

I laughed. "OK. I know you spend *every*
Thanksgiving with the Carson clan. I know it's not fair.
And I'd support you in bucking any other family
tradition. I really would. But I just think you'll lose so
much more than you'll gain if you aren't here for
Thanksgiving. On account of it being Julie's day. Why
don't you compromise? Leave Thursday evening, and
ask your folks to celebrate Thanksgiving on Friday this
year."

Ivy was quiet. "Do you really think it matters that
much to her? I mean about Julie's birthday?" she asked
finally. "Or is it just that she doesn't want her control
over us broken?"

"I really think it's Julie's birthday," I said firmly.
"Some folks hold on to what's theirs so tightly, they
never stop grieving, Ivy."

Her eyes were blue. Blue like the sky is today." It was Thanksgiving. Daryl was celebrating with my family rather than spending the day at a boarding school he loathed.

"Whose eyes were blue?" We were sitting in the kumquat tree, bellies bulging and defenses down.

"My mother."

"Your mother?" I had met Daryl's mother at the beginning of school. She was a small woman with a dour expression and hazel eyes.

"Cynthia isn't my mother."

I waited.

"My mother's name is Lyla. Lyla. It sounds like a flower, doesn't it?" He looked at me, the longing in his eyes so fierce it took my breath away. He looked up at the sky again. "All I remember of her is blue eyes, blonde hair, and soft loving arms. She died when I was four."

He reached into his back pocket and pulled out his wallet. "Here she is." I swallowed a bitter lump in my throat, and accepted a worn photograph of a blonde woman with a small boy in her arms.

"I'm sorry." I fought back the tears, but they crept out the corners of my eyes anyway. "I'm so sorry. You look so happy together." The slender woman and the rotund toddler were beaming at each other.

Daryl nodded and put out his hand for his picture. "She drowned in the province." He caressed the edges of the photo with his fingers. Then he placed it back in his wallet, stowed the wallet in his pocket, and finished his story in one breath.

"When I was six, my father showed up at the school one afternoon with Cynthia. 'Daryl, this is your new mother,' he said. 'Kiss your mother.' I've never kissed her and I've never called her mother. He used to spank me for it when he took me back to the province for vacations. Now we all just ignore each other."

He was so intense. We had met only two months before, but it wasn't the first time his intensity had scared me. I couldn't imagine losing my mother at such a young age. But I couldn't imagine resisting my father for 10 years either.

"Daryl, I want to be your friend." That was all I could think to say.

"Hi, friend." He smiled his Elvis smile at me.

"Hi," I said, suddenly feeling shy.

The phone rang back in less than 20 minutes. "Katie?" It was Ivy.

"Yes."

"I've thought about what you said. You're right. Tell Mother Carson for me that the kids and I will leave Thursday evening."

"You're a good person, Ivy McCloskey Carson."

"So are you, Katherine Brandon Carson."

I hung up and dialed Mother Carson's cabin. "Ivy just called me," I said, making it sound as it was Ivy's idea. "She says to tell you they'll leave Thursday evening. Her folks will have Thanksgiving on Friday. She just had to think the whole thing through."

"That's what we all have to do sometimes," Mother Carson replied happily. "That's what we all have to do."

7

One precious half hour alone with Carol's letter before the girls come home. I had saved it until I was certain there would be no interruptions. I hadn't touched the house, the breakfast dishes were still on the table, but I told myself I'd make up for it after snack time.

Out of habit, I went into the upstairs bathroom, locked the door, and sat down on the toilet. My father called it his "reading room," and now that I no longer had toddlers, I understood why. Before then, not even the bathroom was sacred.

Dearest Kate,

When you read this I'll be arriving at my grandmother's in Colorado. You know how she is about long distance calls, so phone as soon as you can. I'll be waiting to hear from you.

I'm tired, dear friend. All I want is to soak my weary body, soul and spirit in your majestic wilderness for a few weeks. Please tell me I can come.

Love Always,
Carol

That's all? I turned the blue flowered stationery over. *Nothing on the back?* "*Please tell me I can come.*" *Of course, she can come. She knows that!* I reread Carol's letter. Something was wrong. The letter wasn't like Carol at all.

From our bedroom, I dialed her grandmother's funny old house in Denver. No answer. I dialed again and let it ring 15 times. Still no answer. *Take care of Carol, whatever it is, God,* I prayed. *She's been doing your work all these years while I've been sitting here. Don't let anything go wrong for her.*

There's only one thing I want to be when I grow up. Rich!" Mayda studied the scrapes and scratches on her arms and legs. "Rich covers it all."

"Why?" I licked a stinging grass cut on my pinkie.

"This trip for instance. We wanted to see what was on top of this hill, so we spent four torturous hours climbing it. If I was rich, I could have just sent a slave."

"There aren't slaves anymore," Carol said righteously. "Besides, money can't buy people and it can't buy love."

"Da da de da . . . " I hummed the Beatles' hit song, "Can't Buy Me Love," lifting my face to the late afternoon sun.

Mayda countered with a full-voiced rendition of another Beatles tune, "Money."

Carol laughed. Then suddenly serious, she said, "I want something else. I want to make a difference. I want the world to be a better place because I was born into it."

I knew what I wanted. I had glimpsed it up on the hill we were leaving. Only I didn't know how to talk about it.

"Can you believe we climbed all the way up this hill

without knowing we could've just taken a bus up the back side?" Mayda grabbed her ponytail and pretended to hang herself by it.

"Think we'll make it home by dark?" I asked.

"Maybe," Carol said.

We looked at each other and grinned, pleased with the prospect of life in general and ours in particular. Then with a holler for humanity and a whoop for youth, we raced each other downhill to the bus stop, arriving just in time to see the back of bus 114 round a corner and disappear.

"Now what?" Mayda groaned. "There won't be another bus for an hour."

Who could tell? Maybe it was fate. Perhaps our adventure had been destined from the beginning to last a bit longer. I hitched myself onto a large boulder and peered to the left through the shrubbery. Something glittered like water in the sun.

"Come on," I yelled. "This day's not over yet." Ignoring our battered bodies, we raced through the grasses again, irresistibly drawn by the possibility that some fool had dug a swimming pool in this deserted place.

Mayda streaked ahead of us as if propelled by some inner message that salvation was at hand. Carol and I followed, soon reaching a bamboo and glass vacation home to find Mayda neck deep in the most luxurious swimming pool we had ever seen.

With Miss Burson far from mind and body, we didn't think to ask permission or even to check if the house was occupied.

Three hot, tired, dirty teenage girls, and one heart-shaped swimming pool full of cool, clear water, could only mean one thing. Without hesitation, Carol and I joined Mayda, flipping, floating, and diving like three baby porpoises.

Mayda noticed him first. He was standing by the edge of the pool, tall, tanned and self-assured. He bent down on one knee and reached out to shake her hand. Little shivers ran up my spine.

"May I introduce myself?" His voice was amused, a faint British accent suggesting an overseas schooling. "I'm Carlos Vega. I'm pleased to find that you've accepted my invitation to join me for a dip in my pool."

Then with a mischievous smile, he set down his drink, whipped off his sunglasses, and did a perfect swan dive off the board.

It felt positively sinful, finding ourselves without warning beside a handsome stranger in his swimming pool. Who knew what might happen? It felt wonderful. Carol and I raced him across the pool and back, while Mayda arranged herself on the sundeck to impress him with her body.

Mayda had a fantastic body. I couldn't argue with it. But I thought it would have looked better in a bikini. As it was, with her dripping cut-offs and T-shirt, I thought she looked more like something the cat dragged in.

She must have looked better to Carlos, I thought as I scooped out the vanilla ice cream. I planned to treat the girls to hot fudge sundaes for snacks. There was something reassuring about hot fudge sundaes. *She must have looked better to Carlos because on her eighteenth birthday, he married her.*

So Mayda had gotten her wish. She was rich. She wrote off and on. Always from some exotic place. I knew for a fact that Carlos didn't use his fingers to push his food onto his fork. Bobby said their life was an oriental fantasy. I told him mine was more an accidental reality.

How strange that life writes such a different story

*for each of us. If I'd gone and arranged myself like a
Barbie doll on that sundeck instead of racing around
the pool like a peasant, would I have married Carlos
instead?* I mused as I heaped on the fudge sauce.

Carol had gotten her wish too. For the last six years,
she had been working on disaster relief with the
International Red Cross. As part of a special advisory
task force, she was first on the scene of crises the world
over.

What about you? I asked myself as Fibber barked
out a welcome to the chattering voices in the front yard.
Midpoint between Mayda, who pleased herself, and
Carol, who pleased strangers, I found myself wondering
what was lacking. I pleased my family. I knew I cared
for them well. But back there on the hill that
glimmered in the sunlight, I had thought there was
something more. Was it something none of us had
found?

The uneasy feeling of something lost before it was
gained followed me through supper. It didn't help that
no one had answered in Denver all afternoon. Seeing
how anxious I was, Bobby offered to clean up after the
meal. As he cajoled three lazy wenches into "beating
the clock," I retreated gratefully to the study.

Carol answered on the third ring.

"Carol! I've been calling all day. What's wrong?"

"Katie, it's so good to hear you." I was reassured by
her calm, familiar voice. At least she sounded like
herself.

"What's wrong?" I asked again.

"Nothing."

"Nothing?"

Carol sighed. "I'm just kind of burned out, I guess."

"Mama Katie's gonna make it all better." I used my
let-me-kiss-the-booboo voice. "How soon can you get
here?"

"Is Wednesday too early?"

"Carol, this is me, Katie. Don't act like a stranger. You know you're welcome any time under any circumstances."

"I'm so glad."

Then I told her about D. J. Costain's will, just to amuse her and take her mind off whatever was bothering her. She laughed and said she'd have to buy one of his books to read on the plane. I almost said they weren't her type, but instead I told her I'd have the answer to my riddle when I picked her up at LAX on Wednesday.

"I love you, Carol," I reminded her before we hung up.

"I love you, too." She sounded relieved to say it.

I sat in the study long after we said good-bye, picturing her clearly in my mind. Wide, honest eyes. Firm set to her jaw when she wanted something done and knew it was right. Slim, girlish figure even at 30.

"Is she OK?" Bobby poked his head into the study.

"She says she's just burned out."

"She works hard in some pretty awful places, Katie."

"I know. I just hope that's all. Somehow, I think there's more to it. She's coming Wednesday."

"Good." Bobby came in, sat down in the recliner by the window, and patted his lap. I went over to him and put my arms around his neck. "Sometimes I envy you, Kate," he said.

I drew back in surprise. "Why?"

"Because of the friends you have. Carol and Mayda. There's a loyalty between you I've never experienced with any of my friends. Not even the ones I grew up with."

"Maybe it's a difference between men and women," I said, hoping to soothe him.

"Not in your case," he replied evenly. "It's the same between you and Daryl."

"I haven't seen Daryl in six months." I laughed awkwardly. "Last time he wrote, he was hunting wild boar in Indonesia. I think he's forgotten me. Anyway, they're all your friends too."

"Yeah." He kissed my neck. "But it's not the same thing. There was something unique about your high school years. Something that gave you the kind of friends few of us ever have."

8

"I want to spend the day in the forest," I told Bobby the next morning as I passed him on my way to the kids' room for a second wake-up call. Breakfast was already on the table.

He nodded. "I'll invite myself to Mom's for lunch."

"Thanks."

"How far are you going?"

"Up to the meadow." It was my favorite spot, a grassy meadow misplaced high in the forest.

"Borrow Gretchen then. Coyotes only laugh at Lhasas."

Later, I walked the girls to school, went by Margie's for Gretchen, and sauntered leisurely into the forest. I walked without thinking, delighting in the trees and the sky and the dogs. I wanted to think, but first I wanted to walk. I wanted to do only one thing at a time, as if by simplifying my life I might begin to understand something I'd missed.

The sun was high by the time I reached the meadow. I chased the dogs—as if I could ever catch them—and fell panting into the wild grass. Stretched out, my feet still telegraphing a running sensation to

my brain, I felt glad for the solidness of the earth. Then
I climbed on a large warm rock, and let myself
remember.

It was our junior year. We were in world religions class
listening to an audio on sixteenth century mystics. Carol
was passing notes to Mayda in front of us, and someone
across the room was shooting spit wads.

It wasn't the subject matter, we just weren't ready to
be cooped up in class. The whole world screamed
through the windows begging to be explored. I turned
in my seat to look at the gentle hills that rolled away
from Hope Academy.

One of them, green and inviting, had my name on
it, calling to me. I stared at it, trying to figure out if the
green was trees or just tall grasses. Popcorn clouds
decorated the blue sky, luring me to come to them.
How to be in school on a day like this?

Just then, it caught my eye. A glint of something
shining in the sun, bright and silvery like tinfoil.
Nudging Carol, I scribbled my question on her
notebook. "What is it?"

She followed my glance and shrugged. Nothing was
supposed to be out there. Hope Academy was at the
edge of Manilan civilization. The glow of adventure ran
warm in my imagination as I waited for class to end.

The mysterious shimmering in the hills beyond us
spiced up our week. Everything from a space
laboratory to a millionaire's mansion ran through our
collective fancy. And when we found out on Friday what
it really was, we weren't disappointed.

I thought to ask Armando if he knew. Bus drivers
knew everything. He said it was a new monastery for a
silent order of monks. With a little reality to build on,
there was no end of spine-tingling scenarios to weave.

And so, the controversy began.

Carol insisted it was a front for the CIA. Mayda was sure it was the Russians or the Chinese. I couldn't believe the blasphemy. I was certain the monastery was just what it purported to be—a new monastery for a silent order of monks.

What would it be like to be always silent? I wondered. *How could one never talk?* Armando had said it was a sacrifice to God. *Why did God care?*

Lunch time came and the bickering continued. Nobody wanted to give in. Then as I bit into my bologna sandwich, I realized it was Friday. "Hold it!" I cut Carol and Mayda short. "Is everyone home this weekend?" They both nodded. "Then let's find out."

"What?" Carol raised her eyebrows. "How? The road turns into a footpath just beyond the school. Want to rent a pedicab?" She laughed, and we joined her at the thought of some poor little Filipino boy bicycling three healthy American girls up the hill in his pedicab.

"So?" Mayda asked when the laughter was over.

I had a plan. Mayda's folks were off saving Southeast Asia that week. When her parents traveled, Mayda was entrusted to the questionable care of Ging whose current amorous preoccupation with the gardener made her highly susceptible to a little careful blackmail. Leaving for the day without disclosing our destination would be easy.

"We'll just have to ride our bikes as far as we can," I said after I told them what I had in mind.

Carol and I got permission to spend the night at Mayda's house, conveniently forgetting to mention to our parents that the Martels were away. We had an honor code that prevented lying, but allowed for selective forgetting.

Friday evening was spent in wild conjecturing amid peanut butter chocolate bars. "This will be the best,"

were my last words shortly after midnight as I fell
asleep praying I wouldn't break out.

The plan was to wake up at six o'clock and make
our way up the hill before the afternoon sun blasted
Manila. Six o'clock came too soon—at least three hours
before it should have. But while I was flexible, perfectly
able to remain in bed at a moment's notice, Carol was
not. In her mind, a plan was a plan.

Dragging me out of bed, Carol and Mayda forced
juice down my throat, and we were off to who knew
what. Halfway down the block, my bike chain came off.
It seemed as if our adventure was a bad idea getting
worse. I pulled my beret over my eyes and scowled at
the neighbor's dog who was doing his thing on the lamp
post.

"Sit down, Katie. And don't say a thing. I'll fix your
chain." Carol guided me maternally to the curb and
quickly fixed my bike.

On again.

Traffic was heavy over the Pasig River, and we
stopped to use the pedestrian walk. I was beginning to
wake up. Halfway across, we rested on the rail to stare
down into the muddy water below. A busload of people
had gone off the bridge last typhoon season. No one had
survived. I imagined the screams and cries for help as
the bus sank to the river bottom.

"Do you think there were any kids on that bus?"
Mayda whispered.

Carol shook her head. It was a busload of people
going to work. We moved silently across the bridge.

Then suddenly, I was glad to be alive. Hopping back
on my bike, I revved up and did a wheelie. It wasn't the
sort of thing to do on a crowded street, but the day was
glorious. A perfect day for adventure. "Last one to the
dirt turnoff is a rotten egg!"

Joyfully, we raced each other down the boulevard,

dodging buses, jeepneys, pedicabs, and pedestrians. It was a day for losing all inhibitions. Half an hour later, we reached the dirt turnoff. The temperature was on its way up, but we thought we could find the monastery by noon if we kept going.

Resisting the urge to rest by the roadside, we passed Mayda's canteen around as we rode along. Carol took a long drink, coughed violently, and spit it out. "Bleech! What kind of poison is this?"

Mayda looked offended. "I'll drink my own lemonade, thank you, if you're going to be so picky." She reached for the canteen, took a swig, sputtered, spit, and made a fish mouth. "Forgot the sugar." She grinned ruefully.

I passed my water around, and we picked up speed, Carol in the lead, followed by Mayda. Physical exertion wasn't my favorite thing. The day was heating up and we'd been at it for two hours. I concentrated on Mayda's back and kept pedaling.

Hope Academy, posed righteously on its hilltop, was the last set of buildings we had to pass. Our silver-topped mystery rested in the hills behind the school. Getting by the school was the trickiest part of our plan. Day students weren't allowed around campus during weekends without permission. Any nosy kid could report us, and discovery by an adult mandated a hasty retreat to plan B. Since there was no plan B, we had to make sure no one saw us.

We rounded the last bend, only to be greeted by a crew of boarding students. They were working on the gravel at the bottom of the hill, and a big dump truck blocked the road. Stopping short, we plopped down on the soft earth to consider this unforeseen menace.

Carol passed out chocolate chip cookies and we finished the water in my canteen. It was clear we'd have to abandon the bicycles. After finishing our snack, we chained the bikes to the fence that separated the road from the rice paddy on our right. Mayda suggested camouflaging them with dried grass and we did our best. It was a little sparse, but it might have fooled a blind man at midnight.

No one had come up with a plan, so we commenced cautiously toward Hope Hill, hugging the fence for cover. "If you can't go up, go down," I muttered under my breath.

"You'll go down—straight down—Katherine Brandon, if we don't think of something quick," Mayda whispered.

I had a plan. Not the greatest, but it would work. I motioned toward the rice paddy and crouched down to wiggle under the fence. We would have to go across the rice paddy and around the back of the school. We would come out by the athletic field and no one would spot us. Mayda looked as if she wanted to throw up, but a parting glance at the road crew told her I was right. She followed with Carol in tow.

Rice paddies are deceiving. Like clouds, they appear to be what they are not. I would often sit in a trance on the edge of Hope Hill hypnotized by the paddies below. Carpets of waving green, their undulating curves whispered sensuously, "Throw yourself down. We would never hurt you. We'll catch you in our soft bed of green."

That's what the rice paddies wanted you to believe, but up close, the magic was gone. They appeared to be ordinary blades of tall grass, whistling in the tropical breeze. What nonsense made you long from the hill to be part of the rice paddies?

Stepping into them, their true nature showed. Mud to your knees—slimy, slippery mud that threatened to eat you if the things slithering across your toes didn't— the tall grass turned into a vicious animal, cutting and biting and hissing at you until you left its domain.

Mayda nudged my back and I gathered my courage.
Good practice if I was ever tortured for my faith.
Holding hands, we walked single file down one long
row of rice and up another. Nobody fell and nobody
screamed. We reached the back side of Hope Hill
undetected with sanity intact.

After climbing the hill on our hands and knees, we
rested under the bougainvillea bush behind second
base. Mayda giggled and I turned to shush her. She
pointed at me and began to howl. Carol looked at the
two of us and joined in.

We were hot and tired. I knew I looked like a half-
baked mudpie. I itched all over. Suddenly, I had a vision
of us knocking on the door of the monastery and
signing to the silent abbot for a shower. It was a prime
situation for teenage hysteria. I knew it was coming.

Then I saw Mr. Weaver. There was no one less likely
to understand three teenage girls looking like feral
children and laughing hysterically under a
bougainvillea bush behind second base than Mr.
Weaver. And he was coming toward us, shovel in hand.

Carol and Mayda were beyond hope. We huddled
together behind the bush, convulsed with silent
laughter, lungs aching for air. Nothing could save us
now. But this adventure was meant to be. Suddenly, Mr.
Weaver dropped his shovel and returned to the
gymnasium.

Composing ourselves, we watched from the cover of
another bush high on the hill as Mr. Weaver returned
with a pair of pruning shears. He picked up the shovel,
walked straight to the bougainvillea bush, and began to
dig. With a quick thanksgiving upward, we continued
quietly up the hill.

I could see the roof of the monastery bouncing the
sun back through the tall grasses that surrounded it.

Mayda was sure there was a pattern to the reflections, an intricate code broadcasting the secrets of the American naval station across the bay in Subic.

9

It was noon. The ordeal in the rice paddies had put us behind schedule, and without our bicycles the journey was longer than we'd planned. The noonday sun in Manila was not a friendly animal. I looked around for a shady spot to rest for lunch, but we'd come to the green I had wondered about and it was all grass, knee deep. No place to stop. No place to sit down.

The caked mud on my ankles itched. The grass cuts on my arms and legs itched. The sweat in my hair and on my neck itched. I turned toward the ocean and lifted my face, searching for a hint of breeze to ease my agony. The dirt in my sneakers and between my toes itched.

Then with a burst of energy that took me by surprise, I bounded up a rock to the left of the little path we were making in the grass. Now I stood above the jungle below. I searched again for a breeze and detected a slight stirring near my cheeks. Something inside my brain exploded.

Whipping off my tennis shoes, I ripped off my T-shirt and wriggled out of my cut-offs. I arranged them neatly on the sizzling rock, seated myself on top of them, reached for my lunch, and crunched on a carrot.

Mayda and Carol were aghast, staring at me in astonishment. But the mood was irresistible. It was the best lunch we ever had.

We passed a lazy half hour, knowing we'd pay for our sins with a sunburn from head to toe. Finally, spirits restored, we guzzled the last water in Carol's canteen and continued toward our destination, dressing as we walked.

I could see the monastery through the grasses as we approached. Stopping to serve as mirrors for each other, we repaired as much damage as possible with spit and a broken comb. Then we stepped out of the tall grass onto the monastery grounds.

That moment remains with me speaking peace to my inner soul where I dwell alone with God. Someone had planted a Japanese garden and it was perfect to the last detail. Someone who loved the earth had labored long and hard to redeem the hilltop where only wild grasses had grown for centuries. Someone who loved had carefully planned every shrub and miniature tree, every winding pathway and sculptured bridge. Someone who loved had filled the garden with sleepy ponds and rippling brooks.

We had promised each other not to break the silence of the monastery, and I clasped my hand against my mouth to still the shout of joy that almost escaped me. Water! Cool, clear, shaded water. And tended grass. Soft and supple beneath my feet.

Hiding our tennis shoes in the wild grass behind us, we headed silently for a circular pond beneath an ample willow that beckoned to us like a mother's arms. I slid my feet into the water and slowly let my ankles, calves, and knees follow. Gently, I eased back on the soft, cool grass and spread my arms to greet the ground that received me.

None of us knew how long we lay there relishing

every soothing sensation. When I turned on my side to look at the garden again, a tall monk was standing by the willow looking down at us. Again, my hand went to my mouth to stuff back the cry of surprise that automatically shook me. I poked Carol and slowly rose to my knees. The monk smiled.

Frantically, I searched my conscious for the greeting we had worked out in sign language before leaving Mayda's house. Horrified that I couldn't remember any of it, I looked pleadingly at Carol. Her brother was deaf and she'd been signing all her life. Carol skillfully cut the air with our prearranged greeting "Good afternoon. We've come to visit you from Manila."

The tall monk's eyes sparkled as he signed back. "I'm glad to have the pleasure of your company," his hands said.

Carol returned the compliment. Then he signed a complicated maneuver I couldn't follow. Something about ears. Carol's eyes grew wide, her sunburn turning purple. She leaned over and whispered, "He wants to know if we're *all* deaf."

"Tell him we aren't deaf. We just don't want to break the silence of his monastery," I whispered back.

Carol relayed the message to the monk who, to our astonishment, burst into hearty laughter.

"Of course. Bless your hearts," he said in perfect English. His voice was deep and woodsy. The rolling *r*'s betrayed a Spanish accent. "How thoughtful of you. But let me assure you that the sweet voices of God's children would never disturb our silence. It is for these gifts from God that we listen when we are silent."

Glorious talking. We began jabbering at once. It wasn't until he slowed us down that our story became understandable and he learned why we had made the journey up the hill.

His name was Father Fernando. He leaned against

the willow and motioned for us to sit down again.
"Well, children," he said kindly as he settled down on
the ground in front of us. "What is it you wish to
know?" He smiled as he spoke, and I felt relieved at the
obvious pleasure our intrusion had brought him.

"Are you the gardener?" I asked, sure that he was.
Father Fernando radiated the same orderly peace that
gently stirred within me as I contemplated his garden.

He nodded slightly, pleased that I had known. We
sat silently, one mind and heart with the beauty around
us.

"Do you know about St. John of the Cross?" The
Father broke the silence.

"We studied him in our world religions class," Carol
answered. "I wish I'd listened better."

"And so you shall." Father Fernando laughed.
"Studies can be so dull when you have no way to
experience them yourself. But now you have come to the
hilltop to see for yourself, and when you return to
world religions, you will listen carefully to compare it
with what you have seen."

He clapped his hands, apparently delighted with the
logic of his little sermonette. "And now. Are you ready
for a tour of our humble home?" He pointed to the
monastery and began to rise.

"Father." I hesitated. There was something I had to
understand before I could go in. "Can I ask one more
thing first?"

"Of course, child. Questions are the food of the
mind." He beamed at me. "Ask away."

"It's about the silence. I don't understand the
silence. Armando said this is a silent order of monks,
and yet you aren't silent and you don't mind our noise.
Are the monks in the monastery silent? And if they are,
why aren't you angry that we trespassed on your
property?"

"Ah, the silence." He beamed again. "Yes, the monks in the monastery are silent. Most of the time." He leaned toward us. "You see, when we think of silence, we think of listening. It takes much practice to learn to listen."

"But Father," I interrupted, "if everyone—or almost everyone—is silent, who do you listen to?"

"Why child, we listen to the voice of God in the things He sends us each day. That is why I am so pleased by your visit. Although we purposely built our monastery on this hilltop away from the hustle and bustle of the city, God has sent us His children today through the inhospitable grasses of the surrounding countryside." Father Fernando smiled, gesturing toward the pile of tennis shoes that showed through the border grasses on the edge of the garden.

"We learn about God as we take time to listen to His world. Most of us are too busy talking to realize that God's world is shouting His love all around us. We have dedicated ourselves to learning to listen to the voice of God built into His creation from the beginning."

He looked at me. "Are you ready now?" he asked softly, motioning to the monastery.

I smiled and stood up. *Who would have thought that silence was listening?*

At the Father's insistence, we scrubbed our tattered shoes in the laundry room, set them in the sun to dry, and began our tour of their living quarters. It was plain and spartan, but somehow comforting. Comforting perhaps to know there were so few real essentials after all. Monks of all shapes and sizes, camouflaged in their long brown robes, greeted us with silent smiles as we moved from room to room.

When we reached the chapel, Father Fernando explained that the monks had built the monastery themselves. It was meant to be small with no more than 30 monks in residence. We listened intently as he explained the history of his order and the present day regulations that governed their lives.

As he talked, I contemplated the cross crafted in stained glass above the altar, marveling at the God who invested Himself in city clamor and country quiet with equal enthusiasm. The same God who had my father preaching earnestly in busy downtown Manila, had Father Fernando listening earnestly in the quiet hillside chapel. It occurred to me that I should never be bored.

We passed through the kitchen a second time. Father Fernando put his finger to his lips playfully, rested his hand on the counter behind the cook, and skillfully stashed half a dozen rolls up his sleeve. Gleefully scooping up a pitcher of water from the well behind the kitchen door, he beckoned us to follow him up the stairs leading to the bell tower. Small concrete benches had been built into the wall and we made ourselves comfortable.

"There." He pointed to a clearing in the distance. "Hope Academy. Now I know. You have been there all this time. Now when I ring the morning bells, I shall ring out a prayer for you in world religions class." He chuckled and passed out the contraband rolls.

A gentle ocean breeze refreshed us as we rested in the cool of the bell tower shade. Looking out over Manila and the blue beyond, I felt as if I could stay there forever.

At length, Father Fernando looked at the sun. "The night will fall on you if I do not send you on your way," he said. "But at the risk of spoiling your sense of adventure, I must tell you that you could have come by bus.

"There is a road that runs behind the hill on the way to the province. Bus 114 comes halfway up. The road from the bus stop is dusty, but straight and free from mountain grasses." He smiled, surveying our cuts and bruises compassionately. "But then, that which is gained through enterprise and hard work is so much more appreciated."

Reluctantly, we descended the bell tower, found our shoes, and after many good-byes, made our way down the road behind the monastery. Father Fernando was right. It was dusty but straight, wide, and trouble free.

I turned back to look at him standing at the edge of his garden, still waving good-bye.

"Wait a minute, gang," I said, fingering the mother-of-pearl cross my father had given me for my fourteenth birthday.

Turning quickly, I ran back up the hill, slipping the cross off my neck as I went. Then reaching up to kiss him on the cheek, I carefully dropped the necklace into one of his big pockets. "Thank you again, Father," I whispered, returning to join my friends without waiting for his reply.

10

retchen and Fibber cornered a squirrel on the edge of the meadow, bringing me back to the present with their frenzied barking. I listened to them for a moment, tired of it, and hopped down to pull them away while the little animal escaped.

Back on the rock, my reverie disrupted, I wondered whimsically what I'd do with the money if by some twist of fate D. J. Costain had made me his sole heir. Then the dogs, hearing something beyond my range, quivered with good will and dashed into the forest to greet someone. Soon Bobby stood waving beneath a scraggly pine, struggling against Gretchen's full-bodied affection.

"May I join you?" he called.

It was a question with only one answer, but I was glad he had thought to ask. "Just get your ticket at the gate," I called back, trying not to betray that the intrusion wasn't welcome. I had wanted this day to be all mine, to squander as I pleased. *He knew that when I left this morning,* I told myself as I watched his strong legs confidently devour the field, *so he must have a good reason for coming.*

Then I wondered if something was wrong. One of the girls perhaps. "What's wrong?" I asked anxiously as he came up to me.

"You tell me," he said solemnly.

"Are the girls OK? You didn't come because something's wrong with one of them, did you?"

"No, don't worry. I came because of us." He smiled sadly.

"Bobby, there's nothing wrong with us."

"I came because of you then."

I waited silently, wanting him to speak to me, to say something that would touch the restlessness inside.

"You're so distant, Kate." He stood in front of me, blocking the sun. "Ever since school started again, I feel as if I'm losing you. This is the eighth time in six weeks you've come out here to the meadow all by yourself."

"You've been counting?" I stared beyond him into the forest. He wasn't saying anything, wasn't telling me anything that made a difference.

"I love you, honey. What's going on inside you? I want to help." He lifted my chin.

"Would you leave Fallstown if that's what I needed?"

I didn't look away, but Bobby did. He took his hand from my chin and sat down beside me. "I can't talk to you, Katie," he said with a sigh.

"Yes, you can." Suddenly, I didn't want to spare him. "You can talk to me. You just can't listen to me. Bobby Jay, look around you. You have everything you want. And you just can't hear that it isn't enough for me."

"I love you so much." His voice caught. "When a man and a woman love each other, it's supposed to be enough. They aren't supposed to need anything else."

"You sound like a country and western singer," I said sharply.

He stood up, walked away, tossed some sticks to the dogs, and came back. "Then what is it?" he asked, legs firmly apart, as if gripping the ground for support. "What is it you want, Katherine?"

"Don't. Don't draw a line and put us on opposite sides as if we were enemies. It's not me against you."

"You're right. I have everything I want right here." He spoke slowly while his body stiffened. "But you say you don't. You want something more. What is it? What's going to make you happy? Do we have to move to Southeast Asia and work in refugee camps or what?"

"I won't talk to you like this," I said, panic in my voice.

Bobby softened, and sat down.

"I don't know what I want, Bobby Jay. That's the problem." I reached for his hand. "There's nothing wrong with your life. There's everything right with it actually. Fallstown is a wonderful dream. You're right to love it so."

Words weren't working for us, so we just sat there together. *That's what he assumes. That's what his mother's afraid of,* I thought. *That I want to join some cause like my parents. If only it were so simple.*

I'd kill myself first. I'd rip out my heart, slit my wrists, and spread my blood all over Manila before I'd come back here or anywhere as a missionary." Daryl clawed dramatically at his chest and wrists.

"If you ripped out your heart, you wouldn't have to slit your wrists," I observed.

"Duh! The point I'm trying to make is that missionaries are egocentric, paranoid racists who have no business coming over to another culture, telling people how to live their lives."

I'd been elected party chairman for the junior class, and hoping to rouse Daryl from his studied apathy, had appointed him as my assistant. Now we were spending study hall period outdoors to plan an upcoming fund raiser for the junior-senior event. Sitting next to each other on the bluff overlooking the athletic field, we had digressed from our assignment.

"I'm not going to fight with you," I said evenly. "I don't want to be a missionary either."

"Good!" He wiped his forehead with exaggerated relief. "Then marry me and run off to Zanzibar with me where we'll live out the rest of our lives in pursuit of hedonistic pleasure."

I laughed. "I don't want that either."

"Then what do you want?" He feigned exasperation.

"To be connected," I said thoughtfully. "It's like there's a part of me, deep inside, that's only half born."

Daryl started to tease, then realizing I was serious, simply nodded. And I knew he felt it too, a well of desire, fearful in its ambiguity.

"How about you? What do you want?" I asked.

My friend hesitated.

"Seriously," I said. "Tell me. I want to listen."

Daryl kicked his heel against the dirt. "I want to see everything, do everything there is to do," he said vehemently. "I want to be obligated to no one, absolutely in control of my own life. And I want to die young, accidentally, doing something most people wouldn't dare."

His answer took my breath away, but I didn't show it.

"Do you think that's wrong?" he sneered. "Do you think it's not *Christian* enough? Are you shocked?"

"No, I'm not shocked," I said carefully, knowing from past experience the best way to soothe him. "Anyway, I'm your friend, not your judge. I try not to confuse the two."

Then he changed, suddenly tender. "You're the best friend I'll ever have," he said, taking my hand in his.

"And on our graduation night, I'm going to kiss you."

"You're what?" I drew back in surprise, not knowing how to respond. Daryl teased me constantly, but from the beginning we had guarded our friendship, instinctively certain that amorous explorations would destroy it.

"Just once, on our graduation night, I'm going to kiss you. I don't know what kind of a kiss it will be." He stopped to consider it.

"Not animal, please."

"No definitely not animal. Sweet, lingering, filled with exquisitely restrained passion."

We both laughed.

"Because I love you, Katie Brandon, more than I love anyone else alive on this earth. I'll never spoil that love by romancing you, but I want to kiss you just once. Then when I die, I'll feel your kiss on my lips and I'll be happy because, in my lifetime, two beautiful women have loved me."

He spoke it, searching the sky because he couldn't look at me. And I received it, aware I was listening to his naked soul. Then we planned the fund raiser, knowing we wouldn't talk like this again until graduation night.

A penny for your thoughts." Bobby leaned over to kiss me.

"If they were worth only a penny, it would be a waste of time to listen to them." I responded as I always did to an old saying I considered inane for inflationary times.

"Tell me because you love me then."

"I was thinking about the time Daryl and I planned a fund raiser for the junior-senior event," I said reluctantly, but truthfully. Sharing my unrehearsed thoughts was one of my least favorite things.

"You do that a lot lately," he commented.

"Do what?"

"Fade off like that. Are you always thinking of old times when you fade off?"

"Bobby, your life has been a cohesive whole." I tried not to sound impatient. "Your life has been made out of one experience—Fallstown. Even the four years you spent away at college, you had no doubt you were coming back here.

"My life has been chopped up into little pieces. First Vermont, then Manila, then Westmont, then here." I wanted to add that I wasn't sure I had really chosen any of them, but I knew he would misunderstand.

"It's Daryl, isn't it." It was a statement, not a question.

"Didn't you hear what I just said?" I almost yelled. "It's not Daryl. It's me. There's something I can't define. Something that tantalizes me, but always eludes my grasp. I feel it most often here now. In this meadow. Something haunts me here. It's almost as if there are words hovering in the air, but at a frequency my ears can't hear."

"Do you love him?" Bobby asked.

"I've always loved him," I said. "From the first time I saw him, I loved him. But it's not a marrying kind of love. You know that, Bobby. You know there's no reason for you to be jealous of Daryl. How often do I see him anymore? Twice a year if I'm lucky. Daryl's gotten what he wanted out of life. He's done more and seen more than anyone should expect in a lifetime. He doesn't want to be married to me any more than I want to be married to him."

"It's not the Daryl I know that I'm jealous of," my husband said slowly. "It's the one I didn't know. The one you keep locked inside your memory. The one you just can't let go."

11

Bobby and I walked home together, hand-in-hand, seeking reassurance in each other's touch since words had failed us. My friendship with Daryl was something my husband had learned to accept, but I knew he was still threatened by it. *Maybe that's why he sees a homewrecker behind every other pair of jeans,* I thought now.

Carol and Mayda had been bridesmaids in our wedding. But Daryl was diving for pearls off the northern coast of Australia, and had only phoned the morning of the ceremony. I was foolishly in love then, not just with Bobby but with love itself, with the ritual of marriage and having a home of my own. It didn't occur to me to prepare my sweet new husband for my complicated old friend.

When Daryl showed up in Fallstown to congratulate us three months later, Bobby wasn't ready for his new bride's intense friendship with another man. He wasn't ready for the obvious pleasure Daryl and I took from each other's company.

When Bobby left for work in the morning, Daryl and I would be in the greenhouse talking. When he returned for lunch, we'd still be there. By the time he came home at the end of the day, we might have moved to the living room, but the delight on our faces in being together was still there.

I was young and inexperienced then. I hadn't learned to make my husband feel special in small ways, like tidying the house before his return. Now I always did it, even if it meant whizzing through like a whirling dervish only 15 minutes before he came home.

So my husband had made an uneasy peace with the man he considered competition. I was sure Daryl's macho exploits the world over hadn't made it any easier for Bobby. I never questioned who I wanted as my husband and the father of my children. I knew I hadn't married him on the rebound. I knew he had been my choice from the beginning. But when Daryl blazed in, and Bobby watched his wife and daughters light up like Christmas bulbs, it was hard for him to remember he was the fire that kept their hearths warm all year round.

Still, we were the family Daryl came home to. Once or twice a year and always at Christmas, he blew in like a tall ship from the Orient, bearing gifts and seeking respite from the roustabout life he courted. My daughters greeted their "Uncle Daryl" like a fairy tale prince, so tan and handsome and with so many stories to tell. And my husband tried to welcome this Pied Piper, grateful that at least he was a rover who soon grew restless in one place.

"Let's have a fire." I squeezed Bobby's hand as we stepped out of the forest onto Oak Tree Lane. A fire in the hearth, soft music, and warm mulled cider was our family's favorite way to feel close. "We'll play Christmas music."

"In October?" Bobby smiled at me, knowing how much I loved Christmas music.

"Late October," I said. "Almost November. And I always start Christmas music in November."

He pulled me close and hugged me tight. Then we chased each other inside, tidied the house together, and sat in the kitchen to wait for our tribe.

"What is it?" Susie asked as soon as she saw us side by side at the snack bar. "Why's *he* home?"

"It's his house. Can't he come home early if . . . " I started to tease, but noticing her eyes and recognizing panic, I finished gently, "We just wanted some time to talk."

She drew her shoulders up defensively. "About what?"

"Susie."

"That's the way it happened for Marilou," she explained.

"What happened for Marilou?" Bobby put Missy down and turned to Susie.

"The divorce?" I asked, already guessing.

She nodded. "Marilou came home from school one day and her daddy was home, just sitting there with her mommy like you are. They said, 'Marilou, we have to tell you something,' and she just started screaming."

"But sweetheart," I reasoned. "Marilou knew her parents weren't happy with each other. They fought all the time. She started screaming because she knew what they were going to say. Daddy and I don't fight. We get along fine. There's no reason for you to even worry about divorce."

"Come here, princess." Bobby reached down and scooped her up. "We're going to have a fire tonight. How's that?" Susie buried herself in his embrace, while the other two clamored for equal time.

Mary Ellen called as we stretched the girls' bedtime past eight o'clock, curled up together like a giant octopus on the rug in front of the fire. Bobby disengaged himself to answer the phone. "It's Gabby," he said, stringing the study phone out to me.

I reached around Missy to bring the phone to my ear. "Yeah?"

"I just got this week's *People*," Mary Ellen's words came out in staccato.

"I'm happy for you."

"It's got an article in it about you-know-who."

I had to think for a moment. "D. J. Costain?"

"The very same."

"Any pictures?"

"He's a mystery man, remember. No pictures of him, ever. It's an interview with his agent. They've got a good picture of the agent though. And there's something in here you just won't believe. Katherine, you're absolutely going to die! Die and be buried this evening!"

"What?" I couldn't imagine anything that would live up to Mary Ellen's enthusiasm.

"I can't tell you over the phone. I've got to come over and show you."

I hesitated, looking over at Bobby and knowing he wanted to make love as soon as the girls were tucked in. "She wants to show me something in *People* magazine, something about D. J. Costain. She says I won't believe it."

"Tell her to come over," Bobby said immediately.

"Come in half an hour," I told Mary Ellen. "We'll have the kids in bed by then."

All three wanted to stay up to see the magazine. "In the morning," I told them, trying not to rush them to bed. But my curiosity was growing, and I found myself whisking them through their prayers as if this would hasten Mary Ellen's arrival.

Bobby and I were perched on the couch like anxious children when she arrived. "Here it is! You're not going to believe this!" She flipped open the magazine to the center section, quivering like a puppy in its first snow. "This is his agent." She pointed to a small bearded man in a homburg. "And this is you." She pointed to a painting beside the bearded man.

I grabbed the magazine from her and read the caption. "D. J. Costain, writer of over 60 romances, had one mysterious woman in mind when he wrote them all. Scott Wellen, his New York agent, says he painted her from memory and used her as a model for all the women in his stories. A careful search of Mr. Costain's writings under his three pen names bears out that all his heroines had this woman's extraordinary eyes."

My eyes leaped to the copy beside the photograph. It was a short article, occupying the left fourth of the center page spread. "Scott Wellen knows, but won't say, who this mystery woman is. He won't say who she was to D. J. Costain—friend, lover, sister, wife, or stranger only glimpsed from afar.

"As mysterious as Costain himself, who wrote under the pseudonyms of Dominique Cardin for romances, D. J. Carpenter for adventure/mysteries, and D. J. Carrington for how-to books, is the woman who haunted his days and nights.

"Perhaps the world will never know who D. J. Costain really was. Even after his death, his agent is legally bound not to reveal his true identity. 'The most I can do is to show you this picture,' Wellen says.

"'D. J. was my dear friend and partner, a man I greatly respected and whose passing I deeply mourn. He was obsessed with his privacy, and if after his death, the world finds out the identity which he so successfully hid in life, it won't be from me.'

"There are no pictures of Costain, but we at *People* magazine ask our readers: Have you seen this beautiful woman with the unforgettable eyes?"

The photograph lavishly occupied most of the centerfold. It showed Scott Wellen posed casually next to an antique rolltop desk in a comfortable office. Beside him, a large oil painting on an easel seemed to fill the room.

There was no doubt about it. The woman in the painting, the 'beautiful woman with the unforgettable eyes,' was me.

12

a far back as I can remember, strangers
remarked on my eyes. "Such a beautiful child,"
they'd tell my mother. "And those eyes." At one
point during my sensitive youth, I considered
sunglasses, reasoning that not even a blind girl could
feel as different as I did.

In a time when I wanted nothing more than to be
like my peers, I was different. I was beautiful. But I
wore it awkwardly, not knowing what to do with this
gift I hadn't requested. Later, I used my beauty as a
weapon to take what I wanted. Lately, I had forgotten
about it, knowing I no longer needed to fear or to
worship it.

Now there I was—in *People* magazine. The oil
painting was beautiful, sensitively and lovingly worked
under the artist's hand. But the woman who was being
touted as the "mystery woman," the woman who
"haunted the artist's days and nights," was Katherine
Brandon. Just me. Simply me.

"Let me see." Bobby put out his hand.

I held back, but Mary Ellen, eager to show off her
incredible discovery, took it from me and sat down

beside him, eagerly spreading out the magazine on his knees.

"It's you," Bobby said, amazement in his voice. "It's you, Katie. When?"

I knew he was asking when I'd posed for the picture, but Mary Ellen spared me. "Don't you see?" she said impatiently. "Katie doesn't know! I mean it's like she said at first. D. J. Costain saw her someplace, probably a long time ago, but Katie stayed in his mind.

"He painted her from memory, held her in his mind, modeled his heroines after her. And now that he's dead, he wants to leave her this painting and thank her for inspiring him all these years. It's so romantic! It's like one of his novels!"

Mary Ellen hugged her arms and waltzed around the room. "To think things like this happen in real life." She turned to me. "Thank you for letting me know you, Katherine," she said reverently.

I tried not to laugh.

"If he never actually met her, how'd he know who she was?" Bobby asked suspiciously. "How'd he find her address?"

"You'll find that out on Monday because he's left her a note or something telling her all about it," Mary Ellen said impatiently. "Bobby, it's *so romantic,* and you don't need to get jealous or anything. The man's dead. Can you imagine how rich he was? At least five of his books were made into movies. Rich people hire private investigators and find out anything they want to know."

She turned to me. "You've never worn this gown have you?" She pointed to the crimson gown that graced the firm white shoulders in the painting. "Tell Bobby you've never worn it."

"I've never worn it," I said truthfully, tossing a log into the fire and praying my hands wouldn't tremble. It was true. I had never worn the gown I'd designed for my high school graduation party.

Bobby seemed to be satisfied. Whether he still had doubts I didn't know, but he read the article out loud with enthusiasm now, allowing himself to be swept into Mary Ellen's charade. If the threat of D. J. Costain didn't exist because the man was no longer alive, then the compliment D. J. had paid me was a compliment to Bobby as well. I could see Mary Ellen's fantasy appealed to the cowboy in my husband.

Rumors were flying when we reached the school after climbing the hill in the rain. The boarding kids knew something we didn't know, but as I walked from my locker to my first class, groups of whispering students clicked off like alarm clocks the moment I came near.

Marilyn brushed past me, her nose in the air. Then Cappie Stark, a friend of mine in the eleventh grade, drew me to the railing and told me, "Daryl's been expelled from school for good this time."

"Where is he?" I didn't ask why. I didn't want to hear the story from anybody else. Cappie hesitated. "Where is he?" I grabbed her sleeve.

"He's in the boys' dorm, but you can't—"

The boys' dorm was off limits to girls at all times, but I didn't care. They could expel me too. Handing my books to Cappie, I turned and ran down the stairs, almost colliding with Mr. Donner, the school principal.

"Katie, I wanted to—" He reached out his hand to stop me, but I ducked past and ran on.

The door to the room Daryl shared with five other guys was open. He was sitting on his bed gazing out the window, his suitcases on the floor beside him. I stopped short as I came to the doorway, but he didn't turn around to see who had arrived.

"Daryl?" I hesitated as I came up behind him. He

didn't move, so I kept coming. "Daryl, tell me what happened." I sat down beside him, resting my hand on his knee. He took it and ran his fingers over my fingertips. "Daryl?"

"They finally got me, Katie," he said in a monotone.

"For what?"

"After all these years in this hellhole, I'm not going to graduate. A month away, and I'm not going to graduate." He laughed, a dry crackling noise that assaulted the silence of the big room. "Old Donner finally got me."

"You've been expelled before," I said softly. "You always got back in."

"Not this time, Eyes. Not this time."

"What'll your dad say?"

"I talked to him last night on the phone. I'm 17, Eyes. He says I'm on my own. He doesn't care."

"He can't just abandon you like that!" I said.

"He already did, a long time ago." Daryl stared at the floor.

"What happened? Did you really do something so bad?" I sounded like a child pleading with a parent to promise everything would be all right.

He shook his head. "Maybe. Maybe not. But I'm not going to defend myself. I can't. If I did, they'd fire Flossie. Hope Academy is just a school I've been trying to get a degree from. They owe it to me because I've been stuck here all my life." His voice was so bitter, it made me cringe.

"But Hope is Flossie's world. I won't let them take it away from her. She's the only decent thing about this place."

"Miss Burson?"

Daryl nodded.

Just then Mr. Donner burst into the room. "Katie, go to class," he commanded sharply. Daryl's body stiffened, but he didn't turn around.

"I'll go in a minute." I stood up and faced Mr. Donner, my voice calm and controlled.

"You know the boys' dorm is—"

"You may stand outside the door and time me, Mr. Donner," I said, choosing my words carefully. "I will leave in a minute." I looked him directly in the eyes.

Obviously flustered, Mr. Donner started to speak, decided not to, and marched to the door. "One minute," he said, lifting his left arm in front of him and counting the seconds.

"Who's coming for you?" I asked Daryl quickly.

"I'm taking a taxi to the Meekers."

"No, you're not." Bernie Meeker was a silent, unsympathetic man who represented Mr. Coomb's mission agency in Manila. It might have been a logical place for Daryl to go, but it definitely wasn't the right place. "You'll take the taxi to my house. I'll call my father right now." Daryl didn't answer, but I knew he would obey me.

"I need to use the phone in the office," I told Mr. Donner as I marched past him.

"Katie, you're late for class," he said harshly, glancing at Daryl and then back to me.

"Then it won't matter if I'm a little later." I heard my voice as if it were an echo, crisp and confident, unlike the shaking inside.

The rest of the morning was a blur. Carol and Mayda stayed close, shielding me from the whispers that followed me. By noon, I was physically ill and called my mother to come for me. Daryl was waiting in my room when I got home, and we walked out to the kumquat tree to talk.

It was a long story, believable to me only because I knew Daryl lived by his own rules. Still I didn't fully understand what he was telling me. Somehow Miss

Burson had become more than just a mother/teacher figure to him. He had written her letters filled with his anger, his hopes, and his love for her. The secret he would never betray was that they had been reciprocated.

"Mrs. Kraemer found my letters," Daryl said slowly. "She searched Flossie's bedroom. We had agreed to burn our letters. It was dangerous to keep them. I burned hers, but for some reason she kept mine. Mrs. Kraemer took my letters to Mr. Donner.

"Old Donner jumped on them like a barracuda. He called us both into his office, threw the box of letters at us and said, 'Explain this.' I thought Flossie was going to die. She just sat there, turning pale.

"Donner says, 'Have you seen these before?' Flossie just nods. 'Then explain them.' She doesn't say anything so he looks at me and says, 'Did you write these, *Mr. Coombs?*'"

"I say, 'Yes, I did *sir*.'" Daryl's voice could have soured milk.

"He says, 'Explain.' So I did. I told him I'd written them because I was in love with Miss Burson. I told him she had tried to talk me out of it, had told me to get counseling, had asked me not to write her, and had never returned my affection.

"Then the scuzbucket turns to Flossie. 'Is this true?' he asks, as if it's an interrogation. Flossie looks over at me, and I send an unspoken message that there's no point in ruining her life too. Then she straightens up in her chair, puts on her 'Miss Burson look,' and says, 'Yes, it is, Art.'

"'Then why did you keep these letters?' he asks. 'It's more to the point to ask you why another faculty member searched my room,' she says in a heat. 'I've been at Hope Academy since its inception. The least I expect is to be treated like an adult.'

"She dug her hooks into Mr. Donner and turned the inquisition around." Daryl grinned wryly, remembering Miss Burson's performance. "You should've seen her, Katie. Flossie really gave it to the old buzzard good."

When Daryl finished, I could only say, "It's not fair! It's not fair for you to take all the blame."

Daryl turned to me, a frightening and unfamiliar fierceness to his voice. "It's not your place to say what's fair. This is my decision. I live by my own rules. No one else will ever know what really happened between Flossie and me. No one. And if you can't accept my decision . . . " He didn't finish his sentence. I don't think he dared.

"I'm your friend, not your judge," I said, straining at the familiar words to make them ring true. "But I don't understand, Daryl. I mean I understand why you're doing it, but I don't understand why she's letting you. If she really loved you, she wouldn't. But I'll always stand by you. Always."

Daryl put his arm around me and pulled me close. "You're one in a million, Eyes," he said. "One in a million." Then he laughed a dry laugh. "Flossie doesn't love me, and I don't love her. It was just a game. Something to do because it hadn't been done before. A taboo to be broken. Something you'll always be too innocent to understand."

13

By the time Mary Ellen left, Bobby was in a festive mood. "There are no pictures of Costain, but we at *People* magazine ask our readers, have you seen this beautiful woman with the unforgettable eyes?" he quoted, catching me around the waist. It was almost more than I could bear. "Yes, I have," he went on. "I've seen her, and she's *all mine*."

"Bobby, don't." I imagined him licking his lips, a longed for pastry finally n his possession.

"You'll have to get used to it, honey. Do you know how many people read *People*?" He let go of me, picked up the magazine, and flipped to the front. "Doesn't say, but it has to be millions." He whistled. "Millions of faithful readers are going to be looking for you, Katie," he teased. "Where will you hide?"

"Bobby!"

Realizing I wasn't pleased, he changed his approach. "Does it scare you?"

I nodded.

"It's a compliment."

"I know." I started for the spiral staircase. "But it makes me feel weird." I stopped on the first stair and turned toward him. "How would you feel if you saw your picture in a magazine above the caption, 'Can you identify this handsome stud? Linda Lust, writer of over a hundred sleazy romances, has to know who he is. Readers everywhere. Can you help her find him?'"

Bobby barely hid his amusement. "It's not that kind of painting, honey," he said, holding the photo out toward me. "It's beautiful. D. J. was a gifted artist. I hope Mary Ellen's right. I hope he left you the painting."

Then he contemplated me with soft lights in his eyes. "You're breathtaking, Katherine," he said. "Not just in the painting, but in real life. Standing there, you're so beautiful. And you're mine."

I lounged against the railing for a moment, posing for him so he wouldn't know I really wanted to run, to turn back the clock, to hide from the fear that only tightened its grip on me.

"Turn off the lights and come on up," I whispered, knowing what was expected of me. Strangely, I wanted to give it, to have life go on as it should, to prove to myself that nothing was wrong.

Upstairs, Bobby stood behind me in the darkness, gently massaging my shoulders. "Let's make our little boy tonight," he whispered. "A ten pound baby boy with the most beautiful mommy and the proudest daddy in the world." I had climbed the stairs to sit by our window, looking out at the stars and thinking how cold and lonely they looked in space. Now Bobby was urging me toward the bed.

I turned to him, feeling small and fragile in his embrace, wanting to melt myself into him, to become so much a part of him no one would ever find the real Katie Brandon again. "Let's not talk about the painting anymore tonight," I pleaded. "Let's just forget about everything except you and me."

Bobby pressed his lips against mine, and for the next hour I was lost in his pleasure. *I've succeeded in reassuring my husband,* I thought as I stared at the ceiling, listening to the even rhythms of Bobby's sleep. *Now if I can only reassure myself. Where can he be? How could I get a hold of him before Monday? How do you get in touch with a man who's hunting wild boar in Indonesia? There must be ways to locate missing people overseas. But in two days?*

Put it here, partner." I held my hand out to Daryl. We had arranged the junior-senior event down to the last detail. Now we planned to sit back and watch it roll by.

"It was a pleasure." Daryl pumped my hand, stepped back, and bowed. I responded with a curtsy. Then we hugged each other gleefully. We had come up with a shining plan that promised to become a legend at Hope Academy, passed down from class to class like the tales of Jimmy McWheeler, the first graduate and consummate practical joker.

Our fund raising efforts had been a success, netting us more than enough to finance the going-away bash for our rivals. After years of us-against-them and who's-better-than-who, the junior-senior event was our last chance to demonstrate our superiority. In the weeks that followed this traditional rite of passage, the seniors would be untouchables, consumed with the formal graduation festivities that ushered them off into a bittersweet sunset.

The metamorphosis that would overtake the senior class in the weeks to come was something we juniors could only guess at. A long summer still had to pass before we took their places as kings of the hill. The importance of the junior class party chairman, therefore, could not be overstated. On his or her shoulders rested the honor of the rank. Daryl and I were sure we wouldn't let our classmates down.

The junior-senior event could have been anything— a weekend trip to the golden shores of Matabunkay, an excursion to the waving rice terraces of Banawe, a restful repose in Americanized Baguio. But we settled on a ball, the likes of which had never been seen at Hope Academy or, we imagined, would be glimpsed there again.

The whole weekend must be filled, of course. So parties had been scattered strategically, swimming parties here, bowling parties there, sensitively arranged for small selected groupings. But on Sunday came the *coup de grace,* the final triumphant of elegance, the Grand Ball at the Presidential Hotel.

I had been "going with" Steven Nolte that semester. Although love had died, at least for me, it was too late to find another date. Daryl was madly in love with Connie "Sugar" Beals, so I couldn't use him for a substitute. Anyway, Steven was easily the best looking guy in the senior class. I dressed for the ball imagining that Paul Newman was coming for me.

Steven "Newman" Nolte rang the doorbell promptly at six. Steven could drive, lucky woman that I was, and I settled into his dad's Pontiac like Cinderella in her carriage. *An evening where nothing can go wrong,* I told myself.

Surrounded by sloping lawns and cascading waterfalls, the Presidential Hotel greeted us like a travel poster for steamy oriental nights. A warm Asian breeze wafted about my earlobes, teasing the hair piled high on my head, as Steven opened the door and took my hand. I wanted to die because I knew I'd found heaven.

People began arriving at seven o'clock. Carol, Mayda, and I whispered furiously about the gowns and tuxedos as each couple stepped through the ribboned archway. Tasteful and elegant mingling ensued, followed by a sumptuous banquet replete with black tied waiters and non-alcoholic champagne. Then the dancing—honorable, dignified, scarcely touching dancing. And last of all, the selection of the King and Queen of the Grand Ball.

Each junior and senior cast two votes in a secret ballot, one for king and one for queen. When the votes were tallied by Mr. Donner, my gorgeous steady, Steven Nolte was king, and his lovely queen was the fair-haired, full-bodied Amy Rose.

Daryl and I had come prepared. Leading them into a side room, we dressed them in royal accoutrements, rolled a red carpet up to the bandstand, heralded them out to a majestic march, and bestowed them with their crowns.

"Now King Steven and Queen Amy will hold court for their royal subjects," I announced into the microphone, feigning boldness lest my trembling voice betray me. "They are present before you to grant gifts to their humble people. I have here in my hand a basket full of requests."

I held up a small white basket. "These requests are within our regents' power to grant this evening. Members of the junior and senior class may come up one at a time, choose a card, read the item listed on the card, and receive it with blessings from the royal hands. Men will make their requests to Queen Amy, women to King Steven."

Everyone clapped, delighted with the unexpected ceremony. I had coached Carol and Mayda. Carol was to be first, with Mayda saving her turn for a time of mass timidity. Carol swished up to the bandstand, reached into the basket, pulled out a card, and asked King Steven, "As a souvenir of your coronation, grant me an item now on your person, not normally worn in the water." King Steven blessed her with his watch and a warning to "take good care of it."

Paul Steffel followed eagerly with the same request, and received a long white glove from Queen Amy. All went lightly while the King and Queen still had outer accessories to give, the assumption being that the petitions would soon change and become more probable. But they didn't. There was, in fact, only one request in the little white basket. "As a souvenir of your coronation, grant me an item now on your person, not normally worn in the water."

While King Steven and Queen Amy had only their ball garments to give, the color of Mr. Donner's face began to match the yellow candlelight that flickered at each table. King Steven relinqui ned his tuxedo jacket, cumberbund, and shirt. Queen Amy gave up her lace and sash. Mr. Donner now matched the rose carpet.

Nervous laughter, spurts of giggling and this-can't-be-true snickers filled the room. Everyone waited. Finally Mayda pranced up. "As a souvenir of your coronation, grant me an item now on your person, not normally worn in the water," she read off the card, curtsying to King Steven. The room fell apart as he slipped off his trousers, handed them to her with cool dignity, and stood before the court in his dark boxer shorts.

Mr. Donner matched the red tablecloths. Pushing his chair back abruptly, he jumped to his feet, glaring in my direction as if looks could kill. Then Miss Burson went into action. I had stationed her near the principal and now she pushed him back into his seat, whispered in his ear, and smiled at me. Reassured, the teachers and students turned back to the royal couple.

Daryl strode up to Queen Amy, asked the familiar request, and received her clinging evening gown. The court roared. The sovereigns, red-faced but dignified, remained calm, avoiding eye contact with superior grace. The court clapped and cheered, assuming their royalty had passed the supreme test.

"Hail King Steven and Queen Amy," Daryl, Mayda, and Carol began chanting on cue. But I stepped to the microphone, held my hand in the air, and announced, "Just a moment. There are still two cards left in the basket. Two members of the junior class haven't been granted their wishes. Bonnie and Chet, come on up together." In the back, Bonnie Adams and Chet Short, the shyest couple in the room, tried to fade into the hotel decor.

Led by my three friends, the court clapped and stamped until Chet and Bonnie sided up to the bandstand and in trembling voices repeated the fatal petition. "As a souvenir of your coronation . . . " Chet faltered just behind Bonnie.

Steven and Amy appeared to be stunned, looking hesitantly at me, turning distinct shades of pink, and proceeding at my enthusiastic encouragement. Off came the dark boxer shorts and the dainty chemise.

To reveal, of course, matching swimsuits.

14

Carol, Mayda, Daryl and I stayed after the Grand Ball to supervise the cleanup, which meant our dates stayed as well. Although Carlos hadn't been introduced to her parents, Mayda was already "married in her heart" to him. Nevertheless, she had accepted a tremulous invitation for Skippy Prine, the class worm, puffing him up to boa constrictor in the process. Now, after such a stimulating evening, she wasn't in a hurry to ride home in a dark cab with him.

Carol and her date, Hutch Cummings, were a matched set, the nicest guy and girl in the junior class, the "perfect couple." Their longstanding romance was nearly platonic, however, so they didn't mind staying either.

As Daryl and I rolled up the red carpet, I glanced over at Steven and Connie. King Steven was tuxedoed again, but from the way Connie looked at him, I could tell she still saw him in his bathing suit. "Look at Sugar," I whispered with a faint nod in her direction.

"She looks great," Daryl said, eyeing her from the neck down.

"Yeah, she's got a terrific face," I said sarcastically. "I mean look at the way she's oogling my boyfriend."

"Jealous?"

"Hardly. Are you?"

Daryl shrugged and tucked the carpet under one arm. "Who can fight hormones?"

"Do me a favor?" I asked, quickly plotting a subterfuge to end a nagging relationship.

"Sure."

"Let her go home with the King." I would ask Steven to take Connie home and then break up with him in the morning for being unfaithful to me.

Daryl felt his chin for stubble and thought it over. "What if I lose her? I've only had her two months. Joe had her for five and it was murder to pry her away from him."

"So? Kenny had her six months before Joe, and Sandy five months before that. She's a long-term relationship. She won't break up with you after only two months. It's not her style. She's too loyal."

"You really want to get rid of old Steve that bad?" Daryl knew what I wanted out of the favor without being told.

I nodded. "He's talking about staying here and going to U.P. after graduation so we can 'still be together.' It isn't fair to string him along."

"OK, ask him to take her home. But I wouldn't do it for anyone else."

"I know." I smiled and blew him a kiss. The perfect end to the perfect evening. The greatest difficulty in my life had just been resolved. "This won't take long," I said. "I'll be right back."

True to my word, it didn't take long. All King Steven and Sugar needed was a polite hint that the cleanup might take longer than either of them deserved to wait. "Thanks, old man," Steven said as Daryl handed him

Connie's wrap. "I'll take good care of her."

"I expect you to," Daryl said gruffly.

"You be my witness," I whispered as the spare couple left the room. "He was absolutely drooling over her."

Daryl stared longingly at the exit doors. "Yeah, drooling."

"Let's get this over with." I waved at Carol and Hutch who were removing the centerpieces from the tables and storing them in boxes. Then I strolled over to the bandstand, strumming an imaginary fiddle and twanging, "Sugar in my coffee, sugar in my tea, sprinkle a little sugar all over little me."

Actually, the cleanup didn't take long. Since most of it was done by hotel workers, we only had to rescue what was ours and load it up in Hutch's truck. A half hour later, we were finished.

"You're a trickly little deviline," Daryl observed in the taxi home. He was staying the weekend at my house.

"Why?" I asked, assuming an innocent air.

"As a souvenir of your coronation, grant me an item now on your person, not normally worn in the water." He imitated Mayda's whispery voice. "That was your idea. And now sending Steven home with Sugar."

I pretended not to catch his drift. "So?"

"So you're full of surprises." He smiled, touching my cheek with his thumb. "I like that about you."

I smiled back at him. "You're pretty full of surprises yourself."

He shook his head. "Not like you. You look so sweet and innocent."

"You're right," I said. "No one would ever mistake you for sweet and innocent." I had started to tease, but halfway through my sentence I realized I was really saying something. "But you're the reverse," I went on.

"You look and act like such a tough guy, but nice things keep coming out of you. You're full of surprises too. Only the other way around."

Sometime in the early morning, I sank exhausted into a shallow, anxious sleep. There was no way to reach Daryl, no one who would know exactly where he was. He had no other lasting relationships from his long years at Hope Academy and, as far as I knew, none from his life since. His parents were still in the Philippines, and although he was their only child, they hadn't spoken to him in years.

I awoke with a jolt, aware that someone was watching me. "Who is it?" I barked as I sat up. My eyes focused to see it was only Bobby, standing at the end of the bed. "What . . . what time is it?" I asked, feeling disoriented.

"Ten."

I jumped out of bed. "Ten?"

He handed my my robe. "I was trying to decide whether to wake you up."

"What about the girls?"

"I fed them." He grinned. "I know how to do that. I'm not completely helpless without you, you know. They're downstairs watching cartoons."

"I'm sorry," I said.

"For what?" He sat down beside me and held out his arms. "You deserve to sleep in if you want to. You don't have to get up now, for that matter."

"No, I have a million things to do." I snuggled into his chest, my voice muffled.

Actually, I had only one thing to do all Saturday— worry. But I battled it with an autumn version of spring cleaning. Starting in the attic and working my way toward the basement, I cleaned drawers and cupboards with a vengeance. Bobby visited me occasionally to inquire if I was enjoying myself. I responded heartily that I was, and kept working. Around three o'clock, it occurred to me to call Scott Wellen.

Bobby had taken the girls down to the cafe for ice cream. I was straightening the bookshelves in the study when I noticed the phone and realized that Scott Wellen must belong to a literary agency. Being D. J. Costain/Carden/Carpenter/Carrington's agent, the agency was probably his own. The article in *People* magazine based him in New York City.

After getting the number from information, I dialed with trembling hands, my body turning to jelly. A gruff masculine voice answered immediately. "This is Scott Wellen. I'm not in, so you'll have to leave a message." The line was silent, the machine on the other end waiting. Not knowing what to say, I hung up.

"This is Katherine Carson. If you know Daryl Coombs, would you please call me?" *No, that won't work. If he doesn't know Daryl he won't call, so I won't know if he got the message.* "Hello, my name is Katherine Brandon Carson." *No, I sound like a contestant on 'What's My Line?'*

Finally settling on a message, I dialed the Scott Wellen Agency again. After Mr. Wellen's terse greeting, I spoke into his tape recorder. "This is Katherine Carson, the woman in D. J. Costain's painting. I must speak to you." I left my phone number and hung up, feeling like the desperate heroine of a Dominique Cardin novel.

I had moved to the living room and was fishing small toys from the belly of the sofa when my family returned. "Guess what I had?" Missy challenged, licorice pleasure all over her cherubic face.

"Peppermint? Strawberry? Rainbow sherbet? Eggplant? Turkey and stuffing?"

"Eggplant! Turkey and stuffing! Oh, gross!" Missy

wiggled with delight. "It was licorice. I had a double scoop of licorice!"

I hugged her, licorice face and all. "I never would have guessed," I laughed.

"Let's have a picnic. It's a great day for a picnic," Janie suggested.

"Yeah, let's!" Susie and Missy chanted like a Greek chorus.

"I can't." I made a sad face. "I promised myself I'd sort out all the places in this house I don't usually get around to. I won't finish before five." I couldn't admit to them that I also wanted to be near the phone.

"Mommy!" It was three-part harmony this time.

"I'll tell you what," I said, compromising with myself. "If you can talk Daddy into making supper, we'll eat just as soon as I finish and drive down to the movies tonight. I saw in the paper that there's a Love Bug double feature playing."

"Hurrah!"

Bobby fixed popcorn, cheese slices, canned peaches, root beer floats, and pickles. "I ought to open a restaurant," he said smugly as he served his cuisine buffet style. "Call it Dad's Pad. Probably be a chain in six months."

"A chain of what? Gastroenteritis?" I kidded.

"I refuse to be insulted." He passed me the pickles. "This is a balanced meal. Protein." He pointed to the cheese. "Starch." The popcorn. "Vegetable." The pickles. "Fruit." The canned peaches. "Drink and dessert." The root beer floats.

"Of course. A balanced meal. How rude of me not to have noticed." We both laughed.

As we sped down the mountain toward the valley that evening, I could only think of Monday and wonder what it would hold for me. Monday I'd be going down the mountain again. To what? Unless Scott Wellen came

into his office over the weekend and returned my call,
I'd leave Fallstown without knowing if Daryl John
Coombs had a double life.

15

I made coffeecake for breakfast Sunday morning.
Carson tradition dictated a special leisurely
breakfast, enjoyed in the greenhouse before the
eleven o'clock service. Something went wrong with the
cake. It came out of the oven flat and leaden like my
heart.

Scott Wellen hadn't called. I'd listened to the
Ansaphone the night before while Bobby was in the
shower. Four calls were on it, none of them from back
east. Only one of the calls interested me. It was from
Carol.

"I've decided to stop by Wichita on the way to Los
Angeles," she had said. "I'm leaving tonight. I'll be
arriving Wednesday afternoon at 5:30 on United, flight
234. See you then, good buddy."

Why Wichita? I wondered as I cased the freezer for
something to replace the coffeecake. *Wichita isn't on
the way from Denver.* Now I was sure Carol was in
some kind of trouble. *Who's next?* I glanced at the
phone and imagined Mayda, crying to me from the
south of France, spilling out that the perfect marriage
was over.

We were just 30 years old, all of us. Actually, Daryl was 31. Still it wasn't midlife crisis time for any of us. But I wondered about myself. When I drove down the mountain the following morning and found out what was in D. J. Costain's will, would I be plunged into a crisis of a different sort?

Discovering a Sara Lee cake stuffed behind a rolled roast, I pulled it out and popped it into the microwave. Then I took out some frozen grape juice and scooped it into a glass pitcher. *"Parle vous, Frances?"* Miss Bridges had taught Susie's class a whole sentence on Friday. I could hear Susie in her glory, showing off for her sisters in the living room.

"French is the most important language in the world," she told them. "It's the language of fashion. I need to speak it because I'm going to be a model when I grow up. I might not even wait to grow up. I might start modeling next year."

"Odelmay derwareunay aybemay," Janie retorted.

Missy figured it out and screamed with laughter. "In the Sears catalog," she cackled. "Modeling underwear in the Sears catalog."

Susie furiously berated their intelligence quotients and stormed into the kitchen. "I can model next year if I want to, can't I, Mommy?"

I almost asked, "Model what?" but I caught myself. Life wouldn't be pleasant if I sided with my younger daughters. "Why would you want to do that?" I asked instead. "That's grown-up stuff. You're going to have all your life to be a grownup. But you only have a few years to be a kid. So you'd better do kid stuff while you can."

"It *is* kid stuff." She struck several poses for me. "Kids model kids' clothes. Like these kids." She pointed to an ad in the Sunday paper.

"Where?" I pretended not to notice the full-color fashion layout on the counter.

"There!" She jabbed her finger at it and read the copy. "Sheila wears an apricot blouse with a rust pleated skirt. See? Sheila's a kid."

I shook my head vigorously. "No, she's not. She's a midget. All the people that model children's clothes are midgets. They're not real kids, they're midgets."

"Mother!" Susie moved her hands to her hips.

"If you don't believe me, go ask your father."

"Daddy!"

We arrived at Fallstown Community Church just as the organist pounded out the opening hymn. I had planned it that way by running my stocking as we left the house, hoping to avoid pre-service gossip about the will. *Perhaps Pastor West will say something during the sermon that will help me face the music after church,* I thought as we slipped into a back pew.

Fallstown had one church. Residents had three choices: attend the community church, drive 20 miles down the mountain to church, or sleep until noon on Sundays. Father and Mother Carson had helped found Fallstown Community Church, so unlike our neighbors, Bobby and I only had one choice on Sunday mornings.

Outside the A frame church building, an oak sign proclaimed, in Victorian letters burned into the wood, "A comfort in times of need." "This is where we should come to rest from our labors," Pastor West often counseled his flock. I wondered surreptitiously what we had to rest from. Rest seemed to be our labor in Fallstown.

Pastor West seldom said anything I needed to hear. Over the years, I had come to use the hour each Sunday morning to make my grocery list and plan my week— all in my head, of course. Although listening was never required, the appearance of listening was socially imperative.

Once again, Pastor West lived up to my expectations,

imparting no new strength to help me handle my
curious celebrity status. The entire congregation
attacked after the benediction. I coped by smiling
brightly and repeating over and over, "I have no idea."
"Can you imagine?" "Isn't it amazing?" "I go down
tomorrow." "Who knows?" "It's probably a case of
mistaken identity." "Well, it certainly is exciting!" Bobby
and I grabbed the girls and escaped for home just as my
face threatened to crack.

Bobby watched me closely all during lunch. When
the girls left to play with their friends in the forest
treehouse next door, he said cautiously, "You're upset.
All those questions after church upset you."

"No," I lied. "I'm fine. I don't blame anyone for
being curious. I think I'm just tired. I slept awful last
night. Mind if I nap?"

"Go ahead." Bobby stood up and kissed the top of
my head. "I'll clean up the dishes."

"Thanks." My heart went out to him. "Thank you
for being such a special husband."

"Anytime—for you—anytime." He looked pleased.

I carried the serving dishes into the kitchen, kissed
him farewell, and went upstairs. The bed was still
unmade so I crawled right into it, pulling the covers up
to my chin. Outside, the sun danced through the
balding branches, sketching little patterns on the
window. *I have such a good life,* I thought. *What do I
have to be unhappy about?*

I just want him to be able to stay until after
graduation. I don't want him to leave for the States all
alone, friendless and abandoned." Daryl had been with
us for a week, tending my mother's garden during the
day, and kicking back with me after school. Now I was
in my father's office at the church pleading for my

friend's future. I didn't see why he couldn't stay with us until school was over.

"He could go back with us when you take me to the States for college." I hoped I was being irresistible. "Daddy, we're all Daryl has left. Jesus wouldn't just kick him out on the street would He?" It couldn't hurt my case to bring Jesus into it.

My father knew it was true—our family was all Daryl had going for him. Mr. Meeker had bought Daryl a plane ticket to the States, Mr. Coombs had given him the name of a distant relative, and Mr. Donner had sent him his transcripts. Then they'd all returned to business as usual, none of them wanting responsibility for this 17-year-old rebel.

None of them gave him what he needed. I thought as I waited in nervous desperation for my father's decision. *None of them gave him love.* I knew my request wasn't impossible. We had room in our house for Daryl. And my family was leaving for the States the week after my graduation, taking an ocean liner for a much needed vacation.

Daryl could cash in his plane ticket and go along with us. In spite of his outward bravado, I knew he was afraid to go back alone. He hadn't seen America since he was 10, and I wanted him to be with friends rather than be alone and scared.

"Daddy, please," I begged.

My father looked up at me seriously. "Honey, right this minute I'm not worried about Daryl." My heart fell. *Not my father too!* "I'm concerned about him, yes," he went on. "And I would be happy to offer him a home for several weeks and companionship on the trip across the ocean. None of that is a problem for me."

He paused and my anxious mind shouted *but? There's a "but" clause in there. But what?* I gripped the desktop for control.

"Katie, I'm worried about you," he said finally. "This relationship you have with Daryl is so intense . . . "

Oh, no. There he goes. Don't say it. Not you too, Daddy. Don't tell me Daryl isn't good for me. Don't tell me he's a bad influence on me. It isn't true.

"You're a funny girl, Katie. Sometimes you're hard to figure out. And your feelings for Daryl are so complicated—mother, friend, more-than-friend, counselor, alter ego. I don't think you understand your feelings for Daryl any more than I do. You just have them with your remarkable kind of loyalty.

"I can't say I think Daryl deserves everything you give him. He's a very troubled young man. But I know he's never hurt you, and I won't tell you he's a bad influence. I know you've heard that at school, and I know it isn't true. I trust him with you."

"Then what's the problem?" I thought I would perish if he didn't get to the point, the *but*.

"The problem is that you can't take care of Daryl anymore. You can't guarantee his future. You can't make the difference for him. If you were to express a romantic interest in him, if you were to ask my permission to marry him, I would say no. That young man has too much agenda, too much ahead of him that I don't want for my daughter."

"But I'm not asking to marry him," I interrupted. "I'm not in love with Daryl that way."

My father held up his hand. "I know," he said. "For which I'm grateful. And I commend you for your level head and heart. But if I allow you to rescue Daryl now, what about the next time and the next time? Katie, I don't want you to fool yourself into thinking you can save Daryl every time, or be there for him always. You can't. You just can't."

I was quiet, considering my father's words. Then I said solemnly, "I know that what you're saying is true.

And I know I'll have to say good-bye to Daryl when we get to the States. Only don't make me do it now, Daddy."

My father was pensive. I knew he was weighing his response deep inside. Then he stood up and clapped his hands in one big resounding motion. "All right," he said heartily. "Let's get out the Brandon armor and rescue a wayward young man one last time." He took my hand and walked me to the door.

"Thank you, dearest man in the world," I said, standing on tiptoes to kiss him. When my father made up his mind, he was one hundred percent. I had negotiated a little more time for Daryl. And for me.

16

The message pinned to the bulletin board in the kitchen said, "Gone to mother's to make Halloween candy. Come on over if you feel like it." I found it when I wandered downstairs after my nap, and sat down at the bar with a flat Coke Missy had stashed in the refrigerator for "some other time." She disliked the fizz in soft drinks, but regularly felt obligated to try one, considering her preference a disgrace to kid-dom.

The brown liquid tasted like cleaning fluid, but I took it as punishment for my sins and gulped it down. *With Halloween almost a week away, I should be working on their costumes,* I thought. I hadn't even helped them pare down the 50 or 60 ideas they'd been tossing around.

They can always go as early martyrs, I thought in daring rebellion, halfway enjoying the prospect of Mother Carson's imagined disgrace in the community when I didn't sew my fingers to the bone over my daughters' Halloween regalia. Not topping last year's costume was a major sign of child abuse in Fallstown.

My own mother hated Halloween. Every year she

wrapped sheets around us, slapped ketchup and shoe polish on our faces, and sent us out as early martyrs. I laughed out loud as I thought of it. When I was 10, I had taken over my own costuming, but I was never sure my get-ups beat my mother's all purpose idea. Now I imagined the talk around town if I did the same with my children.

"She's all taken up with the will, you know. Doesn't have time for her children anymore." "I hear they're having a bit of trouble. The marriage is rocky. Poor Susannah! She may have to step in to protect the children." "She never did quite fit in up here with her background and all. It's too bad that the children have to suffer, though."

I went back upstairs, sat down by the window, and dialed Mother Carson's cabin. Bobby answered. "Hi, honey. Have a nice nap?" he asked. "Are you coming over?"

"I don't think so," I said, deciding only then. "When will you be home?"

"Mom asked us for supper. You OK?"

"Yeah. See you when you get here, then. I'm OK. I'm just going to take it easy. Read a book or something. Don't let Missy taste too much. She'll get sick."

"Love you."

"Love you too."

I ought to do something with myself, I thought as I wandered through the house, just looking at it, taking comfort from its familiarity. *The girls are in school all day. Mother Carson's more than willing to take them any time. I should do something with myself. Go back to school, get a job, or do something.*

Lately, I had been feeling guilty about my leisurely life-style. The year before I had volunteered part time at the school. It was the first year all my daughters were in school all day. By the end of the year though, I had realized I was there more for security than because I wanted to be an all-purpose gofer. So this year, I'd stayed home.

Fallstown, plethoric in its range of community activities, absorbed volunteers like a sponge. In eleven years, I had served on most activities' committees in one capacity or another. But this year, I'd begged off everything. There was something shallow, so basically self-serving about our goals, as if the security of our life-style was the highest purpose of Fallstown man.

Why do I feel I have to justify my time? I asked myself. *And to whom? Is it anybody's business what I do with my spare time?* I walked into Janie's room, picked up her giant panda from the floor, and placed it carefully on her bed. Then I reached for it again, unable to resist cuddling it in my arms. What I really wanted was a baby.

I had conceived each of my three daughters almost as soon as I realized I wanted a baby. I loved being pregnant, nursing, having a little one so dependent on me. My babies fascinated me, and the first year of their lives, I spent all my time watching them grow. They were 15 months apart, wonderful months, months I could lose myself in the magic of their need for me.

When Missy was six months old, I had expected to have another baby. "At least six," Bobby and I told each other. "Maybe more." But it hadn't happened. Nature had shut off the baby factory. No doctor could tell us why. "Everything's just fine," they all said. "There's no medical reason why you can't conceive. Take a long vacation together, just the two of you. That sometimes does it. You're probably just working too hard."

"That can't be it," Bobby would tell me afterward as we tried to console each other. "He doesn't understand that our life's a vacation, 365 days a year."

One time I suggested a cruise. I cut a "love boat"

advertisement out of the paper and showed it to him. He said, "That's great. We'll rent a cabin up at Big Bear for the weekend and go out in Dad's boat."

I said, "Well, it probably wasn't such a good idea anyway," and tossed the ad in the trash.

"No, it's a terrific idea," he said. "Big Bear Lake is wonderful this time of year. The girls will love it."

What are you sketching?" I joined Daryl on deck, my hair tied up in a scarf against the wind. "Can I see?"

"You *can.* It's *possible*," he teased in his best Miss Burson voice.

"*May I?* I held out my hand. It was a black and white ink drawing. "It's me," I said in surprise. "How'd you draw me? I didn't pose for this." In the drawing, I was seated in a small boat, my hair blowing lavishly in the wind.

"You don't need to pose for me." He laughed. "I can draw you with my eyes closed."

"It's beautiful. *May* I have it?"

"If you really want it."

"I do."

"Then it's yours. Just let me finish it."

I handed the drawing back to him. "How come you don't keep your drawings? You tear them up, don't you?"

"Yeah." Daryl bent down, his pen moving swiftly.

"Why? If I could draw like that, I'd be so proud of it, I'd plaster the world with it. I'd never toss any of it."

"Yes, you would. This isn't any good. Go look in an art museum sometime. My stuff isn't any good."

I objected vehemently. "Yes, it is!"

He finished the drawing and gave it to me. "Anyway, I don't want to leave anything behind." He closed his eyes, leaning back with his face to the sun. "I don't want to leave anything to show I was here."

"What?"

"When I die, I want to die without leaving a mark on the world, not for good or for evil."

"Why? Why not for good?"

He peered at me through tiny slits. "Because every possibility of good has an equal possibility of evil, and who's to be the judge? One man's evil is another man's good. Good in one era is evil in another."

My mother saw the sketch of me that evening and wouldn't part with it. "Daryl, this is the best likeness of Katie I've ever seen! You have a marvelous gift." And for the rest of the trip, I think she hoped he would draw her other three children. But he didn't. It was as if allowing the sketch of me to remain was a slip of character he didn't dare repeat.

"Sketch me again," I said one morning, hoping to at least prod his pen into action whether or not I could rescue the product. We were sitting in deck chairs, side by side, the gentle motion of the ocean liner lulling us toward a mid-morning snooze. I turned my head to look at him.

His eyes were closed. Then his lips parted. "OK." He smiled slightly with his Elvis lips.

"Want me to get your drawing pad and pen?" I got up halfway.

"Nope. Don't need it. Sit back. Close your eyes. And just listen. Ready?"

"Ready."

"OK, I'm going to sketch a picture in your mind. Here goes. Laughing mouth and cheeks and eyes. Friendly open eyes that never hide from me. Soft dark hair falling down to strong tan legs eager to live. Sweet red lips I kissed once for a lifetime. Gentle understanding touch that makes me more than I am."

Neither of us spoke for a long time. Then I said,

"Thank you. That's very sweet, Daryl."

"You're welcome." He reached out his hand for mine. "It's a good thing we land in Frisco tomorrow," he said, pressing my hand. "If I was on this ship with you too much longer, I might ruin your life."

"My father thought we were going to get, you know, heavy breathing on this trip," I said.

"Then why did he let me come along?"

"Maybe he wanted us to get it over with, get it out of our systems. Nobody's supposed to have the kind of relationship we have, you know. I think it's a strain for him, wondering all the time when it's going to explode. He said something like that to me back in Manila."

"You're the only relationship I ever did right." Daryl's voice was husky. "I'm not going to mess it up, no matter what people think."

We were quiet, eyes closed, listening to the sounds of the ship and the ocean. Then I said without opening my eyes, "Hey, Daryl."

"Yeah, Eyes."

"What kind of girl are you going to marry? Do you think she'll be anything like me?"

"No. She'll be fat and ugly for one thing. I don't want to have to worry about other guys hitting on her while I'm not around."

"What else?"

He thought for a moment. "Well, she'll be dumb. I don't want a woman competing with me."

"And?"

"She'll be barren. I don't want to leave anything behind, remember."

"That's sick."

"Thank you. Thank you very much."

17

I heard Bobby's footsteps on the gravel outside, his voice gently urging our daughters on. It was nine o'clock, past their bedtime, and I was ready for them with their pajamas out and their covers turned down. As I opened the front door, I saw Missy was already asleep in his arms.

How fortunate I am, I thought, watching them come up the walk. *I had a good father, and I married a wonderful father as well.* Yet it troubled me. I wondered why I had been gifted with so much goodness. It was a question I had wrestled with since the impressionable age of 10.

We had seen a film in church about war torn countries and starving children. On the screen, I saw a girl my age, holding her tiny sister and crying for food. I came home afterward and held my beloved Meg, my tears for all the children that didn't have enough falling on her chubby cheeks. "Why did God pick me to give everything to?" I asked my mother when she found me sobbing in Meg's room.

"God wants all the children in the world to have what you have, sweet Katie," she said gently. "It isn't

God's will for children to suffer. The suffering in the film is not God's doing. He didn't give you more and them less. He gave all of you everything you need, but Satan has snatched it away from some.

"I wish I could tell you differently, honey, but you're old enough to know. This world is in a battle. There's a war between good and evil going on everywhere. We only have one choice. We can't choose between peace and war for the whole world, but we can decide whose side we're on."

She put her arms around Meg and me. "Sometimes we just have to cry," she said softly. "But then we dry our eyes and go back to the fight, each of us in our own small way, doing the things God shows us to do."

My family stepped inside the warm living room and I took my youngest daughter from Bobby. He scooped up the other two, and we carried them to their rooms. After we tucked them in for the night, we laid side by side on our big four poster bed, fully clothed, holding each other tight.

"There's a war going on, you know," I said, so hushed I didn't know if he would hear me. "Sometimes I think I'm up here on this mountain just because I'm afraid of the battle.

"I feel like I'm hiding out, Bobby. I feel like you're hiding out too. People are dying and starving all over the world. Children are hurting and literally being torn apart. And here we are just protecting what we've got."

It bothered Bobby when I talked like that, so I tried not to. *After all, you wouldn't have the courage to change your life even if you had the power,* I reasoned with myself, *so it isn't fair to load all your guilt trips on your husband.*

Sometimes I couldn't push it back, though. Sometimes I had to say what was buried underneath my logic—that we were wasting our lives up in

Fallstown. I didn't say it in so many words, but that's what Bobby heard and that's what I meant.

Bobby sighed and touched a finger to my lips. "You're upset," he said, repeating his observation of the morning. "All that talk at church did upset you."

"Not just that." I sat up, hugging my knees. "I'm scared."

"About what?"

"I'm scared D. J. Costain is really Daryl John Coombs. I'm afraid Daryl's dead." I said it quickly, running all the words together to get them out before I heard myself speak.

"Why didn't you tell me before?" There was an edge to Bobby's voice.

"I don't know," I said, knowing it wasn't true as I spoke the words. "I do know. I was afraid if I said it— even to you—it would make it true." I looked at him, beseeching him to help me.

"Katie!" He took my hands in his, rubbing them gently to give me courage. "That doesn't make any sense. You know it doesn't."

I nodded.

"Why would you think D. J. Costain is Daryl anyway?" He frowned, his bushy eyebrows meeting in the middle.

"So many reasons, Bobby Jay."

"Give me one."

"The dress in the painting is the dress I designed for my high school graduation." I spoke in a monotone.

"I thought you said you never wore it!" I could feel his tension rising.

"I never did," I said quickly. "I never wore it out or to the banquet or anything. But Daryl saw me in it. At home."

Bobby twisted his wedding ring in a nervous gesture I seldom saw. "It can't be him," he said at length, a final quality to his voice. "Daryl spends his time roaming the globe. You know he does. You get a postcard from him every week or two, always from some outrageous location doing some outrageous thing.

"How would he have time to write umpteen books? And even if he had time to write them, how could a guy who barely manages a postcard handle a book? It's ridiculous, Katie. Daryl John Coombs isn't D. J. Costain even if their initials are the same."

"Bobby, Daryl painted that portrait of me. I know he did," I said, growing more certain as I spoke. "I would have known that immediately if I'd let myself. No one else could paint me like that."

"So he painted it. That doesn't prove he's D. J. Costain. Daryl probably met D. J. somewhere. Maybe they were even friends. D. J. probably liked the painting so much, Daryl gave it to him. Maybe Daryl needed money and sold it to him." Bobby sounded so sure of himself that I chose to believe him. Deep inside I knew Daryl would never give away my portrait, but for the moment, I wanted to live on the surface.

We showered together, made lazy love, and then kissed good night. Just before Bobby drifted off, I turned to him and said, "I want to go down the mountain alone tomorrow. Will you be terribly hurt if you don't come along?"

I expected to feel him stiffen, conveying his displeasure with his body even if his words said it was all right. But he surprised me. "It's OK," he said sleepily. "If you want it that way. But if you change your mind in the morning, let me know. Or if you get down there and need me, just call."

I went to sleep feeling like a worm.

Meggie doesn't feel good. Meggie got sick." My

towheaded little sister looked up at me and stuck out her tongue.

I pretended to check it, then stuffed it back in her mouth. "How did Meggie get sick?" I asked her solemnly.

"She ate worms." Meggie fished one out of her jacket and placed it in my hand. "Like this one." It was still quivering.

"Meggie! How many did you eat? Tell Katie, right now!"

"A hunnerd."

"Count them on your fingers. How many?" I uncurled her fist and held up her fingers. "Count how many worms Meggie ate."

"One, two, three, a hunnerd." She wiggled four fingers. "Meggie got sick. Meggie wants to throw up."

"Mother! Meggie ate four worms. She's going to throw up!"

"Sounds sensible to me." Our mother looked out the upstairs window down into the garden where we had been playing. "Help her, Katie. And then bring me up the kind she ate if you can find one. I'll call Dr. Reston and describe it to him."

Meggie threw up, I covered it with dirt, stuffed the live worm in my pocket, and carried her upstairs. "Meggie if you ever eat worms again, Katie's going to spank you," I warned her.

She seemed to have recovered by the time we reached our mother. "Katie's going to spank Meggie if she eats worms again," Meg informed her.

Our mother nodded. "Mommy will spank Meggie too," she promised.

Meggie seemed pleased to hear this. "Two bodies will spank Meggie if she eats worms," she said proudly, holding up two chubby fingers. "Me will spank Meggie also. Daddy will spank Meggie for worms, and Karl will spank her, and Johnny will too. A hunnerd bodies will be spanking Meggie if worms slide into her jullet."

"That's gullet, not jullet," I told her, trying not to laugh. "Don't let Meggie eat any more worms."

"Me not," she said, eyes wide at the enormity of Meggie's crime.

Sometimes I envied the distance my little sister could put between her good self and her bad self. "Meggie" was responsible for all reprehensible behavior. "Me," on the other hand, remained beyond reproach, unsullied by sin of any kind. I loved her unashamedly, passionately wanting her to remain two years old all her life. But she didn't. She went on to become three, and then four, and five—"Meggie" and "Me" gradually becoming one.

"Weren't you afraid to bring a baby to a foreign country?" I asked my mother on Meggie's fifth birthday.

"Hmmm?" She was frosting an animal cake in hopes of making it look like Snoopy. "Well, Manila isn't exactly the boondocks."

"I'm serious," I insisted. "What if she got typhoid fever or diphtheria or something over here?"

"You got diphtheria."

"I know. What if Meggie had gotten it from me? What if she had died?"

My mother stopped frosting the cake and looked at me carefully. "You're asking why we brought you children over here to a land that isn't as safe as Vermont. Am I right?"

I nodded. "I'm not asking *why* so much as *how* you could do it. I'm asking if you were afraid and how you got the courage."

"Yes, I was afraid." She looked pensive. "I'm still afraid, from time to time. You children are the most precious possessions your father and I have. But it wouldn't make much sense for us to tell God, 'We trust you, God. Take our lives. But don't take our children. We don't trust you with them.' It wouldn't be very convincing would it?"

"Howie Brighton's little brother died of whooping cough," I said.

"Did he just tell you that today?"

I nodded.

"I'm sorry, Katie." She put her arms around me. "I wish I could give you the courage you're looking for. I wish there was a trust pill you could take. But courage and trust only come as love grows. They're a product of a one-to-one relationship with God.

"I'm afraid there's no short cut. But I can promise you that as you let Him love you, you'll see His resources are limitless," she said, returning to her baking. "More than enough to cover your need. But like all spiritual secrets, they're unlocked only through relationship."

18

It rained while we slept Sunday night. The world around us was misty and gray in the morning, the autumn colors muted and solemn. I moved through my Monday morning routine like an automaton, fixing breakfast, dispatching my husband and children, dressing myself for the visit to Atwater and Klein.

The phone rang constantly, every friend in town calling to wish me good luck on my adventure. I answered one last time before I switched on the Ansaphone. It was Bobby, calling from his office. "Stop by before you go down the mountain," he said happily. "I have something here that'll cheer you up."

"I'm just getting in the car now," I said. "See you in a jiffy."

The phone rang again as I put my hand on the front door, but I let the machine answer it. *Whoever it is, they can wait or call Bobby at the office,* I thought, reassuring myself that the school would know to call him if there was an emergency with one of the children.

Bobby was in his usual posture, feet on the desk, when I arrived. "Just a minute," he said into the phone, placing his hand over the receiver. "For just one kiss, I'll make your day." I leaned over, kissed him, and stood back waiting.

"It came to the office with the Saturday mail." He handed me a postcard. "Kevin didn't realize what it meant to you, of course, or he would have called. It was on my desk this morning." He smiled at me. "I told you the old bugger was OK," he said as he went back to the phone.

I stood for a moment, reading the postcard, not caring what it said, only soothing my troubled heart with Daryl's precise penmanship, the perfectly rounded vowels and strong definite consonants I had envied in English class. I wanted to hold them to my lips and kiss them, but instead I beamed my happiness at Bobby and left, reading the postcard for understanding when I got to the car.

"It's been too long," the postcard said. "I can't believe I haven't seen my favorite family since March. Got the girls something extra special for Christmas. Still after the wild pig here in the interior of Kalimantan, but thinking of you constantly. Shall be there at Christmas with bells on. Think I'll stay longer Stateside this time. Kiss my girls for me. Give my best to Bob. And take care of yourself. All My Love, Errol Flynn Jr."

Daryl never signed his postcards with his own name. This year he had been Errol Flynn Jr. The year before, he was Robert Redford. He said it gave postmen the world over something to talk about. I turned the card over to an aquatic scene, flipped it back to his short message, and reread it. Then I drove off, waving to Bobby through the front window of Carson and Sons, my heart lighter than it had been in days.

I struck a deal with Hope Academy for you Daryl." My

father stood in the doorway of the kitchen where Daryl and I were making doughnuts. I knew he had challenged the school's decision not to issue Daryl a diploma.

"What's that, sir?" Daryl asked, unaware of my father's activity on his behalf in the past week.

My father cleared his throat. "I'm on the school board so I called a joint meeting of the faculty and the board to discuss Mr. Donner's decision not to give you a diploma. It was a tough meeting. You've raised some temperatures pretty high, son."

Daryl listened without looking up from the dough he was cutting. My father sat down at the kitchen table, and Daryl traded the round doughnut cutter for a paring knife. "Some of us went to bat for you," my father continued. "The yeas and the nays were evenly divided, and no one was willing to budge. Finally, Miss Burson got up and stated flatly that she would resign immediately if you didn't get your diploma."

"So who gave in?" I interrupted, thrilled with the drama of it all.

"Mr. Donner." My father shook his head and spread out his hands in wonderment. "So the deal is that if you pass your final exams, you'll be given your diploma although you won't be allowed at the graduation ceremonies."

"But Daddy, we've already had our finals. We took them this week," I protested.

"I know, honey," he said calmly. "Daryl will have the next few days to study for them. Then he'll take them in my office. I'll grade them and give him his diploma if he passes."

We both turned to Daryl. He was jabbing the dough furiously with a knife, stripping it into long slices and mincing the slices into tiny pieces. "Daryl?" my father said. Daryl just kept slicing. His knuckles were white on the knife, his lips tight and rigid.

"Thank you for all your hard work, Daddy," I said, coming up to hug him and hiding Daryl from his view. "Just give him time to get used to the idea," I whispered. "The whole thing's hard now. He'll be grateful later."

My father nodded and stood up to leave. "You know what they say about gift horses, son," he said, not unkindly, although I knew he wasn't pleased. Daryl nodded, still slicing.

When my father had gone, he kneaded the tiny bits into a dough ball, pressed it flat, and picked up the doughnut cutter again. We didn't talk about it, but before I left for school the next morning, he asked me to bring home his school books.

Miss Burson handed me a stack of books as soon as I reached my locker that morning. "Is he going to do it?" she asked anxiously.

I nodded, taking the books without looking at her and deliberately searching the inside of my locker for something I wouldn't be able to find until she was gone.

"Katie, can't you look at me?" Miss Burson asked, her voice so sad I couldn't refuse her. I looked up slowly. "I've let you down, haven't I?"

I nodded.

"Daryl told you everything?"

I nodded again.

"You can punish me if you want to," she said, measuring her words. "You can tell Mr. Donner what you know. I won't deny it if you do."

"I don't betray my friends," I said, unable to restrain my bitterness. "It's not my responsibility to tell Mr. Donner the truth."

Miss Burson sighed. "I'm your friend too, Katie," she said. "We have been friends, haven't we? All these years?"

I nodded reluctantly.

"Do you really think it would help anyone for me to tell Mr. Donner?"

I shook my head. I knew there were people it would hurt. Not just Miss Burson. It would hurt all the kids who trusted her. I was no longer one of them.

"Can't you forgive me?" she asked, sorrow rippling through her voice.

"I can forgive you," I said in a hollow voice. "I'm not going to hate you the rest of my life or anything. But I don't trust you anymore. And I don't look up to you. I don't want to be your friend anymore, Miss Burson."

My words were heated now. "There's only one question I want to ask you before I graduate. And don't bother answering because it's just something for you to think about when you're alone with yourself. Are you really a Christian? Because Christians act like Christ.

"Daryl isn't a Christian, he doesn't even pretend to be. Maybe you'd better stop pretending, Miss Burson." Then I shut my locker and left her standing beside it, looking into my words. *I don't know how to sort it out, God,* I prayed as I walked away. *Maybe I'm an awful sinner, but I can't just smile at her and tell her I think it's OK to play Judas.*

"Miss Burson had your books ready for you," I told Daryl as I handed them to him after school. "She was glad to hear you'd decided to take the tests." I almost added that it meant she didn't have to resign, but I bit my lip on the words.

Daryl looked pensive. "I've never seen you hate anyone before, Katie," he said.

"I don't hate her. She asked me if I would forgive her and I said yes. I don't hate her. I just don't like her."

I turned to go to my room, but he caught my shoulder and turned me around. "Katie, don't." He bent down to look into my eyes. "Don't let bitterness get inside you. Don't fill those beautiful eyes with it."

"You're a good one to talk," I said, angry with him too. "You should know all about bitterness."

His fingers tightened on my arm. "It's because I know all about it that I'm telling you not to," he growled. Then he let go of me, picked up his books, and walked away.

I knew I had a choice. I was toying with bitterness. It still hadn't dug its ugly roots deep into my soul, but I knew it would if I let it. I knew Daryl was right. I wondered why it was so hard to give it up. Then I realized that in cherishing my bitterness I felt as if I was somehow righting a wrong. *If only I could,* I thought sadly. *If only I could.*

19

The sweet-voiced secretary welcomed me at the law offices of Atwater and Klein. "You're early," she remarked pleasantly, the clock on her desk only registering 9:45. "Mr. Atwater will be with you shortly if you'll just have a seat." She motioned to a grouping of tan and beige chairs in one corner.

The issue of *People* magazine was on the lamp table. I chose a chair next to it, waited until she left her desk for a moment, ripped out the center pages and stuffed them into my purse. Then I sat back hoping I looked nonchalant but thinking, *That was a dumb thing to do. She's probably already seen the article. Anyway, you can't go around tearing the picture out of all the magazines in the country.*

The first thing I wanted to ask Scott Wellen when I got ahold of him was why he had shown the painting to the press. I wondered if I could sue him for invasion of privacy. Whatever D. J. Costain had felt for me in life, he had protected it so jealously that not even I knew about it. What right did Scott Wellen have to break that? If he was such a "dear friend" of D. J. Costain's, why had he done it?

"Mrs. Carson?" Apparently Mr. Atwater's secretary had called my name more than once because now she bent over me as she said it again.

"Yes?" *She knows I tore the page out of the magazine,* I thought with a touch of paranoia.

"Mr. Atwater isn't ready for you just yet, but he thinks it best for you to wait in his office. On account of the press."

"The press?"

"Yes, someone tipped them off that Mr. Costain's will is being read this morning. They've been on the phone requesting an interview. Mr. Atwater is afraid some of them might show up here."

I stood up like a sleepwalker and followed her through a set of double doors. "It's really most upsetting," she said as we walked. "Only Mr. Wellen, Mr. Atwater, Mr. Klein, and myself know the will is being read today. The four of us have been most professional, I'm sure. I can't imagine how the press found out."

I dug my nails into my shoulder bag. "I . . . I didn't know . . . I didn't know it was supposed to be a secret," I said.

"Well, of course, it's your decision. You may tell whomever you like." She smiled at me as if to reassure me. "If you're ready to handle the press, then there's no problem. We just assumed you would want privacy in this matter."

"I do," I said with conviction. "I certainly do. I have no idea what this is all about. The last thing I want is to talk to reporters right now."

"I understand." She tossed her wavy blonde hair and opened the door to an inner office. "Perhaps one of your neighbors overheard, someone from your local paper."

Not one of or someone, I thought as I sat down in front of Mr. Atwater's desk. *More like all of and everyone.* "I guess my life is going to be hectic for awhile," I said with a sigh. "But it'll blow over. I'll just pick up Daryl's painting and be on my way.

"The press can bug me until they're tired of it, but they won't learn anything about D. J. Costain from me. I never even met the man. Don't worry. I won't ruin anything for the family members."

"I'm sorry I don't follow you, Mrs. Carson," the secretary apologized as she closed the door. "Mr. Costain didn't have any family that we know of. You're the only one mentioned in his will."

An involuntary shudder raced through my body as the door clicked shut on her words. Opening my purse feverishly, I pulled out the center page and the postcard. If Daryl was alive and well across the ocean, why was I the only one mentioned in the will? Surely D. J. Costain couldn't have been that enamored with a painting.

I noted the postmark on the postcard for the first time, September 25. It had been mailed only four days later than the postcard I'd received two weeks ago. I began counting off the days. A month had lapsed since Daryl mailed the postcard, proving nothing about his safety.

Turning back to the painting, I willed it to tell me its story. "Who is D. J. Costain?" I asked in a dry whisper.

I spent the afternoon at the hairdresser's, my long hair soaked in beer and set to dry in tiny ringlets. Our graduation ceremony was to be held in the gymnasium at ten o'clock the next day. Tonight was the night we all looked forward to, however. It was the night of the formal graduation dinner and dance.

"This is a look-but-don't-touch hairdo," my hairdresser told me as she undid the curlers. She coaxed the curls into place on top of my head, pinned and sprayed them, and tucked in baby's breath and miniature roses.

"Don't put too many in, Grace," I coached when I thought she was in danger of overdoing it. "More isn't better in this case."

Grace stepped back to survey it. "Enough?"

I nodded. "It's beautiful. You did a wonderful job."

"You're beautiful." She beamed at me with the pride of creation. "Who's the lucky gentleman?"

"My father," I said. "The boy I was going with can't make it, so I'm going with my father."

"Then he's a very lucky father." She accepted my payment and tip. "Have a wonderful evening!"

"I will." My mother honked outside, and I walked to the car stiffly, the weight of my hair pressing down on my body. "Did you get it?" I asked as she swung open the passenger door for me.

"It's in the back." She motioned to a large box in the back seat. "It's beautiful, Katie. You did a marvelous job. Maybe you'll become a fashion designer after college."

"I thought you wanted me to be a child psychologist." I was pleased that she liked my dress.

"One can always hope." My mother laughed. "But one should never insist."

As we pulled into our driveway, I slouched down in my seat. "Don't let anybody see me," I whispered. "Run inside and make everybody close their eyes. I don't want anyone to see me until I put everything together."

My mother's eyes twinkled, but she didn't tease me. Instead, she took the box, went inside, and called out a few minutes later, "Coast is clear. Come on in."

In the safety of my room, I worked on my makeup for the next two hours. Then I called my mother and witn her help slipped into my gown. It had taken me all year to design it. After running the gamut of fashion ideas from *Vogue, Harpers,* and *Mademoiselle,* I'd finally settled on something none of them offered.

I had asked the seamstress to cut a simple evening gown from a bolt of fine material. The color was perfect with my hair and skin tones. And the low neckline set off my shoulders as the skirt hugged my waist, falling away to the floor.

My mother clasped the gold locket my father had given me as a graduation present around my neck. The matching earrings were already dangling in place. I inspected my nails, found them still perfectly polished, lifted my skirt for my pumps, and stepped back to view myself in the mirror. "It's perfect," I said smiling. I was just what I wanted to be that evening—beautiful.

"Are you coming out?" she asked.

I nodded.

"I'll get everybody in the living room." She ran out, returning several minutes later to usher me out with a "Dum, dum, da, da."

Meggie was in seventh heaven. Karl and John held their noses. My father looked proud enough to burst. Then I realized Daryl was missing. "Where is he?" I asked.

My mother shook her head. "He was here a moment ago. I told him you were coming out."

I knew where he was. He was outside in the dark somewhere, unable to face me. We had planned on this evening together, set it apart a year and a half before as our night. Now it wasn't going to happen. We weren't going to graduate together. Having passed his finals, Daryl had already received his diploma from my father. He had graduated all alone.

"Can I talk to you, Daddy?" I walked over to where my mother and father were whispering to each other. "Privately."

"Sure, Princess. Want to go in your bedroom?"

I nodded. When the door to my room was closed, I turned to face him. "I don't think I ever really meant to go tonight without Daryl," I said slowly. "I don't want to hurt you, Daddy, but I don't want to go. I guess I just wanted to get all dressed up. You know, go through the whole thing of getting ready. But I don't want to be there tonight without him."

My father watched me, silent for several minutes before he said, "But sweetheart—"

"You'll have tomorrow," I interrupted, running to kneel beside him. "Tomorrow you can take pictures and be proud of me and do all that stuff. But tonight—well, tonight is the big night for us kids, the night to remember all four years together. I just don't want to do that without Daryl. Please understand."

"OK," he said reluctantly. "Are you against pictures tonight too?"

I nodded. "I'm sorry to be so awful. Will you do me one great big favor?"

He must have found me hard to resist because he smiled at me in spite of his disappointment. "What one big favor?"

"Will you go somewhere?"

"Go where?"

"Anywhere. I just want you to be gone because Daryl will make me go if you're still here."

"I'll go visit Mrs. Jose in the hospital." He stood up to leave.

"Tell mother for me, OK?"

"OK." He put his arms around me and hugged me, careful not to muss my hair. "You're a funny child, Katherine Jane Brandon. Sometimes a surprising child," he said, backing away and tilting my chin up to search my face. "Sometimes I wonder where you came from."

20

I waited in my room until I heard voices outside assuring me my father was leaving. Then a car door slammed and he drove off into the night. *Daryl's out back somewhere,* I thought as I peered through my window into the moonlit yard. *He won't be around front watching for me to leave.*

Then I saw him, moving low among the fruit trees, coming back toward the house. "Daryl!" I opened the window and hissed to him. "Come on up."

"Katie?"

"No, it's Mother Goose. Climb up to the window and come on in."

"What are you doing here?" He stood below me, looking up, legs spread and hands on his hips. "I thought you just left."

"That was Daddy."

"And why weren't you with him?"

"He had to go someplace else. Come on up and I'll tell you about it." I tossed down a verbal carrot, determined not to fork over any more information until he climbed up to the window.

Daryl was an agile climber, the best coconut tree skimmer in school. It took only a few seconds until he was next to me. "OK, what's this all about?" he asked.

"Mrs. Jose's very sick. Daddy had to go visit her in the hospital."

He narrowed his eyes. "I thought she was coming home tomorrow."

"That's just when a person needs a preacher the most." I tried not to laugh. "The shock of coming home. The trauma of the adjustment can kill a person. More people die that way each year than of typhoid and diphtheria combined."

He glared at me. "You shouldn't have done it."

"Are you mad at me?" I knew he wasn't.

"No. How can I be mad at you."

"Then tell me how I look." I backed across the room, posed for him, and waited. "Would I have been sensational at the dinner or what?"

He stared at me for such a long time, I thought he wasn't going to say anything. "Daryl," I finally coaxed, embarrassed by the silence. "I don't think I look *that* good."

Then he grinned. "I'd have to invent a new word to tell you just how good you look."

"Thank you." I curtsied, pleased with myself. "I just wanted you to see me before I took it off. Turn around while I change."

Daryl hummed the Filipino national anthem while I unzipped my gown, let it fall to the floor, and stepped out of it carefully. I wiggled out of my slip and nylons, threw on some jeans and a T-shirt, and looked for my sneakers. "You can look now," I said. "Help me find my tennies."

He found them under my bed. "Now help me undo this hair." I sat down in front of my dressing table.

"Do you have to?"

"It all goes. I want to climb up on top of the roof with you."

He stood over me, his hands hovering awkwardly above my coiffured garden. "What do I take out first?"

"Do the roses first. Ease them out or you'll hurt me." When the roses and the baby's breath and the pins were all lying in front of me, I took my brush and ran it through my stiffened hair.

"Let me do that." Daryl took the brush from me and firmly stroked the hair that fell down my back.

I yawned. "Careful, you'll put me to sleep."

"Then I'll wake you with a kiss." He met my glance in the mirror.

"Ready?" I asked.

He nodded.

"Then climb on up and reach down for me."

Daryl went out the window, shinnied up to the roof, and reached down for me. As I placed my hands in his, he pulled me up with one even motion and we walked hand in hand to the center where we sat down.

"I've always wanted to go to . . . like Israel or someplace," I said, "because they live on their roofs. They have flat roofs that are part of their houses."

"That's because it doesn't rain much. It wouldn't work here."

"People miss a lot. There's something so satisfying about a roof."

We sat there silently, the darkness around us comforting because it told us we were completely alone. No one would look for us up on the roof. No one would ask us what we were doing or tell us to come down.

Then I asked bluntly, just to have it out in the open, "When are you going to kiss me?"

Daryl backed away, feigning surprise. "I thought maybe you'd forgotten."

"You didn't forget. Why would I forget? When are you going to do it?"

"When I say good night."

"Is that the way it would've been if we'd gone to the dinner?"

"Yes."

"Good."

"Katie."

"Yeah?"

"Can I put my arm around you?"

"You *can*. It's possible. You have an arm. I have a body."

"I've noticed. *May* I put my arm around you?"

I moved closer to him, waiting. "Yes." His arm crept around me, hesitantly at first and then confidently, pulling me to him.

"What would you say if I asked you to marry me?" His breath was warm against my neck.

"I'd say no," I replied truthfully. "Would you ask me?"

"No. No, I wouldn't."

"Why?" I drew away from him as if offended and he looked down at me and laughed. "Why wouldn't you ask me? Don't you love me?"

"Of course, I love you." He pulled me close again. "Why wouldn't you accept? Don't you love me?"

It was my turn to laugh. "Of course, I love you," I said. "But I wouldn't accept because . . . " I chose my words carefully, "because I don't believe love conquers all. I want children. I want a home. I want a marriage like my parents have. You would want to give me those things because you love me, but they just aren't you. We wouldn't be happy together."

"Well said."

"Now it's your turn." I looked up at him. "Why wouldn't you ask me?"

His lips were tight, his jaw set with determination. "Simply because I love you so much. I couldn't stand to hurt you, and I know I would."

"Well said."

"We're just a couple of dumb sensible kids, aren't we?" For a second, his voice sounded as if it would crack.

We were silent again, watching the moon and the stars. The sounds of the city beyond our quiet street, traffic and horns and scattered voices, reassured us that life went on in spite of the turbulence inside us.

"After the cruise, we'll say good-bye," I said, resting comfortably against his chest now.

"I'll always come back to you," he whispered. I could hear his heart beating underneath his voice.

"I'll always be glad to see you."

"I know." He pressed my hand. "When you get married, what will your husband think of me?"

"People marry for better or for worse. You'll be part of the better or worse depending on how he looks at it. What about your wife?"

"I'm not going to marry," he said.

"Are you going to be celibate?"

"I didn't say that."

"It'll never be the same for us," I said. "We'll never be together, friends through everything, the way we've been in high school."

Daryl straightened his back. "I plan to attack life like a fool. Maybe I won't notice so much that way." Then he put both arms around me. "Are you cold? You're shivering."

"No. I just don't like to hear you talk that way. Do you have a death wish, Daryl?"

"What do you know about a death wish?"

"I read a novel where this guy had a death wish."

Daryl laughed. "What did he do?"

"Went around trying to get himself killed."

"Then I don't have one. I'm going to live as long as I

can, and come tripping back to visit you in that white little cottage with the picket fence as long as I can. But when the time comes for me to die, I'm going to die. And I won't shed any tears for life."

We sat up on the roof long past midnight, saying all the things we'd said before one last time, checking each other out to be sure we still understood what was expected, what would be needed from our friendship in the years to come. Finally, we climbed down from the roof.

"Is this it? Are you going to kiss me now?" I looked up at him, a new shyness coming over me. I didn't know quite what to expect. He took my hand and led me over to the kumquat tree. "Now?" I asked.

Daryl placed me in front of him, stepped back as if posing me for a picture, cocked his head from one side to the other, motioned for me to move a little to the left, and said, "Perfect."

Then he came over and wrapped me in his arms, finding my lips with his, and kissed me as I had never been kissed before. His kiss was sweet and tender, respectful and loving. I let myself go, responding to him without reserve. Within a moment, it became passionate, fierce and grasping, and was over before I could understand it.

He moved back from me. "Close your eyes." I closed them. "I've always wanted to kiss your eyes. May I?" I nodded and felt a warm, gentle touch on each eyelid. When I opened them, Daryl was gone.

21

"Mrs. Carson?"

"Yes?"

The office door opened and I turned to see a small man with a brown goatee. He was dressed in a blue three-piece suit with white pinstripes. Except for the goatee, Mr. Atwater could have been a mannequin. *He's hardly Daryl's type.* I took comfort from the thought.

"I understand you are in a great deal of suspense, but I assure you that our firm is only following instructions," he said briskly. He walked over to his desk with no further introduction, picked up a video cassette, and handed it to me.

"Mr. Costain wanted you to listen to this in private." My hand shook as I took the cassette from him, and he dropped his professional veneer for a moment to press both his hands around mine. "I'll be right here if you need me," he said.

"There's a room with a video player through that door." He pointed to an oak door connecting his office with the room to the left. "I'll set this up for you. Take as long as you need, then just open the door and call me. I'll be here. I have plenty to do." He motioned to some papers on his desk, attempting a chuckle. "When you've finished with the video, we can go over the will together."

I stood in the center of his office, not responding to the hand on my back urging me toward the next room. "Mrs. Carson, do you understand what I said?"

I nodded.

"Shall we move to the next room then?"

I nodded again.

Mr. Atwater took the cassette from me. "I'll go put this on," he said as if speaking to a recalcitrant child. "You come when you're ready."

I looked frantically about the room. I wanted with all my heart to fling open the office door, race out into the street, and run until I fell into the ocean. Daryl was dead. I was certain now that Daryl was dead. Instead, I followed Mr. Atwater into the next room.

After demonstrating how to stop and start the machine, Mr. Atwater patted my shoulder, told me "These things are never easy," and left, closing the door behind him. I felt completely alone. *That's how you've been all your life about Daryl,* I thought. *How ironic. Except for your daughters and maybe your mother, you've been completely alone in your enthusiasm for him. No one else has ever understood.* And I knew no one else would truly mourn his passing.

The room was hushed, waiting for me to push the black switch. *How did he die?* I wondered. *Instantly, painlessly or slowly, painfully?*

Then I pushed the switch and Daryl was on the television screen, comfortable and familiar, so wonderfully alive in living color. I sat back with pleasure at seeing him, determined to let the tape play all the way through without stopping it.

"Please forgive me, Katie. I hope my little joke has

been mildly amusing." His deep voice poured warmly over me. "If somehow it went awry, as jokes have a way of doing, and caused you anxious moments, I'm deeply sorry. I just figured there was no good way to send you the news of my death, so I might as well have a little fun with it."

He was standing in the sunshine, a sandy beach behind him, generous palms waving in the breeze. I could almost feel the tropics on my face. "This is 1980, by the way." He flashed his terrific grin, and I couldn't help smiling back.

"I've just been back to see you in your little mountain hideaway, my four women and that bear of a husband of yours. You did right to marry him, Eyes. Bobby's just the man you were talking about that night on the roof. Remember?"

A strong gust of wind blew his hair back from his face and he reached to brush it down with his right hand, his left still holding the microphone. "I could reminisce all day with you, darling, but now that I'm dead, there are things you need to know."

He had never called me darling before, my heart caught at the word. "I'm a rich man, Eyes. I've been writing these books, none of them worth spit, but people buy them anyway. You wouldn't want to read any of them. I don't even read them. I either write them in my sleep or in a drug-induced euphoria, but they sell like apples in a depression. Even had movies made of some of them.

"It started after high school, after we said good-bye in 'Frisco. You knew I wasn't going to my aunt's in Kentucky. I turned in my bus ticket, got a room at the Y, bought a beat up typewriter, and pounded out a dirty story about Flossie. Took me a week. I signed it D. J. Costain, took a bus to New York, walked into Scott Wellen's office, and financed my travels by writing junk for the rest of my life."

Daryl was obviously amused with himself, his lip kept doing his impression of Elvis, and he had to struggle to keep serious. Finally, he just took a moment off to laugh. "I'm sorry," he apologized when he had composed himself. "I know this is a terrible time for you, but this 'writing career' of mine is the joke of the century.

"I've got three pen names. Uh . . . " He had to think for a moment. "Dominique Cardin for romances. D. J. Carpenter for how-to books. No, that's wrong. It's D. J. Carpenter for macho books. You know, adventure/ mystery type stuff. Those were the most fun to write, but don't ever read any of them. They're really raunchy. My soul—wherever it lands—will be mortified if you do. Then there's D. J. Carrington for how-to books."

Daryl digressed for a moment. "I wonder how I died," he mused, wiggling his eyebrows in a Tom Selleck move. "What a wonderful mystery. How did the man on the video player die? I trust it was in a blaze of glory.

"I did it, Katie. I put one over on the whole world. However I died, I left nothing behind. Nothing to prove I was ever here. No one knows Daryl John Coombs. No one cares that I'm gone except you, my dear, wonderful friend. You've been my sunshine, Katherine Brandon Carson, and your three dainty images have been my shining stars.

"My greatest wish was to keep the love we shared, to hold it lightly so it wouldn't die. No one else got through to me. I don't know how you did it, but you did. And I couldn't bear to lose you. Don't cry for me, Eyes, now that I'm gone. It all worked out. I lived my life by my own rules. I got what I wanted. I never willingly hurt you or alienated you. It all worked out."

He was quiet for a short while, staring off beyond

the camera to the ocean. Then he shook himself slightly and raised his microphone. "On to business. These guys behind the camera don't speak English. I told them I was from *Newsweek* magazine. They think they're filming a report on these islands. The only person who knows I'm D. J. Costain et al is my agent, Scott Wellen. He's under contract not to reveal my identity. If he does, he loses five of his 15 percent of my take.

"Oh yeah, Atwater and Klein know, of course. But they're lawyers, they can't spill it. I arranged all my financial affairs to pass on to you in the best way possible. Atwater and Klein will take care of everything for you. You've probably noticed they're sort of uptight, but I checked them out thoroughly. They're the best.

"You'll need to get to know Scottie. He's out to make a buck if he can, but he's honest. You can trust him. Just don't let him intimidate you. I probably left books that haven't even reached the bookstores yet. If he can think of a way to publicize my death without breaking his contract, he'll do it to promote the books. Sit on him if you have to. You're the boss now, Eyes. Scottie has to obey you if he wants to stay in the game.

"The money's all yours. Remember when I told you my aunt left me some dough and I asked you to co-sign with me on some papers since I was out of the country so much? Well, your signatures are on all the right places. You're a rich woman, darling. Spend it any way you like. My greatest pleasure in making it was thinking that one day you'd be spending it.

"But don't let it ruin your life. I hope the press doesn't trace you down, but if they do, stonewall them. Don't talk to them. Don't tell them anything. After awhile, they'll find some other chicken to pluck.

"I was a decent businessman. I made some solid long-term investments that you'll be wise to keep. Atwater and Klein will advise you as more royalties

come in. Bobby has a decent head for business too. He'll
tell you what to do with the green. Listen to him. Take
his advice. Don't let the money ruin your marriage.
Money's great if you control it. If you don't, it isn't
worth squat.

"Well, I guess that's it." Daryl had been serious,
intense while discussing the money. Now he seemed to
feel shy, not quite sure how to end. "However I died,
darling, I died thinking of you." He paused and the sun
went under a cloud, or else I just imagined a darkness
coming over the screen.

"I hope you don't mind my calling you darling. I've
always called you that inside my mind. Forgive me for
indulging myself now, but it feels so good to say it to
you. When you explain to Susie, Janie, and Missy that
I'm gone, please tell them how much I love them. Even
in death my love goes on.

"And thank you for your kiss." He put his fingertips
to his lips, held them there as if feeling that long ago
touch, blew me another on the wind, and was gone, the
television screen blank and lifeless.

Daryl John Coombs was gone.

22

aryl is dead. The words hung in my mind like a dreadful foreboding idea, but didn't reach into my emotions as truth. *It's a bizarre joke,* I told myself. *Daryl's bizarre idea of a joke.* And unwilling to humor his ghoulish prank any longer, I shut off the machine and opened the door to Mr. Atwater's office.

"Are you ready?" Mr. Atwater looked up from his papers.

"It's a joke, isn't it? I asked hopefully. "I don't think it's at all funny." I could hear the anger in my voice now. "Why?" I remembered it was almost Halloween. "He's sick. His mind snapped and this is his idea of a Halloween prank. Where is he? What hospital is he in? I'll go to him right away."

Mr. Atwater shook his head sorrowfully. "Sit down, Mrs. Carson, please. May I call you, Katie?"

I nodded.

"Katie, Mr. Coombs made that video tape in 1980," he said with a gentleness that surprised me. "I'm very sorry, but your friend is truly dead. He had an accident in the waters off Kalimantan on the twenty-second of September."

I shook vigorously, not just my head but my whole body. "That's not true. He's coming home for Christmas. He always does. He just wrote." I searched for my purse on the floor next to me and pulled out the postcard.

"See. Look at the date. He wrote to me on the twenty-fifth of last month!" My voice rose uncontrollably. "It's all a mistake. OK, I believe he made the tape in '80, but he's not really dead. He just wrote to me."

Mr. Atwater frowned, taking the postcard from me. "I have the death certificate and a letter from Mr. Wellen, his agent." He turned the postcard over. "Mr. Coombs must have written this postcard and given it to someone who mailed it on the twenty-fifth not knowing of the accident. I'm terribly sorry."

Mr. Atwater's words fell on me like driving rain on a tin shack. The noise was terrifying, but nothing penetrated my defenses. "It's a misunderstanding," I said certainly, my voice unnecessarily loud. I stood up to leave, searching for the way out with inexplicable difficulty.

"Perhaps it would be best to read the will later." he said. "Give yourself some time."

"I don't think that will be necessary," I said. "Daryl will sort all this out when he arrives." Somewhere inside, I knew I wasn't rational, but I couldn't afford to listen. It was too costly, so very costly.

"Take this." Mr. Atwater handed me a brown envelope. "It's a letter from the man who was with your friend when he died. The envelope is addressed to you. Perhaps I should call your husband to come for you."

"No, I'll be just fine. Thank you very much for your time. I'm sorry . . . "

"Mrs. Carson."

"Yes?" I stopped with my hand on the doorknob.

"The press is outside. I must insist that you leave by a side door. It would be unforgivable to allow you to step out front in your condition."

"Thank you, Mr. At—," my bottom lip trembled, and I pressed on it to quiet it, "water. You have been very kind."

"You're my client now, Mrs. Carson." He opened the door for me and led me an unfamiliar way which seemed twisted this way and that. "Any time you need me, just call." Then he opened a door to a back parking lot. "Perhaps you should take a walk, have lunch somewhere, and come back for your car later. I'll be here all day if you want to talk."

The late morning sun warmed me as I stepped out into it. The sky was clear, puffy white clouds decorating the blue. *Nothing's happened to Daryl,* I thought, taking comfort from the normalcy of the world around me. *Misunderstandings like this happen all the time.*

We'll laugh and laugh about this when we get together. 'Eyes, I really had you going that time, didn't I?' he'll say. And I'll say, 'Me? Are you kidding? When do you think I was born, yesterday?'

Remembering Mr. Atwater's suggestion, I crossed over to a coffee shop on the corner and went inside. I would prove to the world that everything was fine. A white-aproned waitress handed me a menu as I sat down in a booth.

"Nice day out," she commented as she placed a glass of water in front of me.

"Beautiful," I said, my voice sounding weak and far away. "Beautiful," I tried again, sounding no better the second time.

The floor and the ceiling of the restaurant seemed to be competing with each other for space. The pink and purple carpeting shouted angrily at the beamed ceiling for room. Then the tabletop rose, pressing me against the booth, crushing my chest and breaking my heart.

Light from the hallway streamed into my darkened bedroom. I opened my eyes slightly to see my parents' figures silhouetted outside my room. My father bent over my mother, listening. Then he entered my room quietly and sat down beside my bed.

"Katie," he whispered, testing to see if I was awake. "Can you hear me?"

I nodded weakly.

"Mommy tells me you can't swallow anymore. Is that right?"

I nodded my head again, motioning to a cup in my hand that held the saliva I couldn't swallow. He kissed my forehead gently and left, closing the door to a crack.

Later voices pulled me from a fevered sleep. "If you can't help her, I'll find someone who can!" My father sounded angry, as if he were struggling to control his voice.

"Stan, I'm telling you it's just the flu. She'll be fine in a couple of days." It was Dr. Wetzel, the doctor we'd seen since we arrived in Manila.

"You said that four days ago. The girl can't even swallow! She has a hundred and four temperature. It's not just the flu." My father was yelling now.

"She can't swallow?"

"I told you she can't swallow!"

"At all?"

"She can't swallow at all. How many times do I have to say it?"

"Stanley, keep your voice down. You'll wake Katie." My mother's soothing tones worked their comfort on my father, and the group by my door moved away.

"Katie." Someone was always waking me up. Why couldn't they just leave me alone? It was Dr. Wetzel this time. "Katie, wake up. I need to culture your throat. Can you open your mouth for me? Here, I'll help you. It doesn't have to be wide."

"Open your mouth, honey." My mother lifted my head and shoulders up from the pillows and I must have opened my mouth because Dr. Wetzel jabbed something down my throat.

Then I went back to sleep, dreaming of frightening things I couldn't understand or remember from one dream to the next.

"She's a lucky one. Another day and you would have lost her." Voices pulled on me again. This time I wanted to cooperate, I wanted to wake up. "It's an interesting case. She's had all her shots. How she contracted diphtheria is a mystery."

I didn't recognize the voices and it was too much trouble to wake up. *I don't mind sleeping except for the dreams,* I thought as I slipped back into them.

"The fever should have broken by now. It could be there's something else we haven't caught."

I didn't recognize that voice either. Besides, I was getting used to the dreams. They weren't so bad if I didn't fight them, if I just flowed with them. They weren't so bad. I knew they could take me deeper where those voices wouldn't keep waking me up. It was the voices I had to get away from now, not the dreams.

"You've got to listen to me carefully, Eyes. Nobody's allowed in here. Not even your parents. They've got bars on your window like a jail. You're quarantined in a hospital that's got guards around it. Eyes, listen to me because somebody's going to find me pretty soon and kick me out.

"Every kid at school had to be innoculated again because you have diphtheria. But they've given you the antidote so you're supposed to wake up now. Only you're not waking up so they have you in this place because they think something else might be wrong with you.

"Eyes, you've got to wake up because if you don't wake up you'll die or you'll fry your brain or something horrible. Now I can understand that you might not want to wake up. Your parents might understand too if they had to. But Meggie would never understand.

"You've got to wake up for Meggie. If you die, you'll ruin Meggie's life. I know because it happened to me. You can't do it to her, Katie. You can't die. You can't ruin Meggie's life."

I can't ruin Meggie's life. I've got to get rid of the dreams, push back the darkness. I can't die because Meggie wouldn't understand.

Y̲ou're right, Daryl. I won't die for Meggie's sake. But how come you went and died on my little girls?"

It's not the same thing, Katie. They have you and Bobby.

"But they won't have you anymore. They won't have you, Daryl John. What right did you have to go die on them? How come you had to be so one way all the time? If you can die, I can to. So there."

Two wrongs don't make a right, Eyes.

"Platitudes."

If you die now, I'll kill you.

"You already did, Daryl John Coombs."

Fiddlesticks! You just get out of that bed and go back to your little girls. You just stop feeling sorry for yourself, Katherine Jane Brandon Carson. You just stop all this nonsense. I'm dead and you can't come along. It's final. You simply can't come along.

23

B obby?" My throat was dry and I couldn't tell if I'd whispered his name or merely thought it. I tried to call him again, but nothing came out. I could smell him. I knew he was there beside me.

"Katie? Did you call me?" His voice sounded hushed, hopeful. I imagined that I moved my head. I tried again, this time sure I had accomplished it.

"Open your eyes, honey. Can you open your eyes?" I opened them a fraction, but they were too heavy for me. "Nurse, she's awake now. She just opened her eyes.

"You're going to be fine, sweetheart. The girls send their love. Don't try to talk. Just rest. I'll be right here. I'm not going to leave you. You're going to be just fine."

I could tell by his glad voice that I'd done something wonderful, I'd made him happy. *That's good,* I thought. *Bobby's happy. That's good.*

The next time I woke up, the weights were gone from my eyes. Opening them, I focused against the artificial light, and found him asleep in the chair next to my bed. "Bobby?"

"Huh?" He stood beside me in a flash.

"What happened?"

"You're in the hospital, honey. You've been sick."

"What kind of sick?"

He hesitated, not knowing how to answer.

"Did I have a heart attack?"

"Yes, but only a mild one." He sat down, tenderly taking my hands in his, willing me to understand. "Remember the doctors in Manila told you the diphtheria weakened your heart?"

I nodded. "What day is it?"

"Tuesday."

"Yesterday was Monday?"

"Yes."

"The Monday I went to the lawyers?"

"Katie." He lifted my fingertips to his lips.

"It's OK, Bobby. I know he's dead." I ran my tongue over my lips. They felt cracked and swollen. "I'm not going to fight it anymore. Only don't tell the girls yet, OK?"

"OK, sweetheart."

I don't think it's funny. You shouldn't have done it, Daryl. You could have killed yourself." Our family, minus my father, was spending the summer in Baguio, mercifully sheltered from the rabid Manilan heat. Daryl had come up for a week, and we were comparing our summers.

"That's the whole point," he argued. "I dove from the cliff precisely because I could have killed myself. I wouldn't be sitting here bragging about diving into the local swimming pool from the high dive, would I? The element of risk makes it exciting, alive. And anyway, I didn't die. I'm right here beside you."

"Some day you're going to kill yourself," I warned sternly. "And you'll have no one to blame but yourself."

"'To every man it is appointed once to die,'" he

quoted, yanking up a handful of grass and scattering it into the wind.

"Ah ha! 'And after that the judgment.' Got you on that one, smart aleck." I shook my braids and made a la-de-da face at him.

"Dum, da, dum, dum. *THE JUDGMENT.* Here come the judgment, here come the judgment."

"Aren't you afraid of it?"

"Nope."

We were seated above the golf course at the military base in Baguio, the summer capital of the Philippine Islands. Everyone who could afford it, journeyed to the mountain resort in the summer like souls finally moving out of purgatory.

The military base was lush and green, the 18-hole golf course among the pines its main attraction. A couple teed off below us, the woman slicing to the right. Daryl whistled and broke into a laugh. The man sliced to the left, and the cat gallery applauded.

"Why aren't you afraid of the judgment?" I pulled a pine needle through my teeth, and waited for his answer.

"Because I don't believe in it." He considered his words, surprising me with the time he took before continuing. "And I don't believe a good God is behind all the pain in this world. But if the Bible turns out to be true and I stand at the judgment, I'm not going to be ass enough to defend my opinion.

"I'll just bow down and confess I was wrong. I'll ask God to forgive me. If He is a good God, He won't toss a repentant sinner into hell. And if He's a bad God, heaven will be hell just like earth is so the whole thing will be academic."

"I didn't realize your theology went so deep," I teased, a little in awe of his logic.

"It's not deep at all," he said sincerely. "Not deep at

all. You might as well know I've tried to believe. Over and over I've tried to believe. I've stayed awake nights trying to believe. But I just can't. There's something inside of me that won't let me. I just can't believe. But Jesus—if He still exists, and if He's divine—knows that. He knows I would believe if I could."

Daryl was so intense as he spoke that I could only wish for words to comfort him. Then a foursome teed off, and he whistled for them, clapping and shaking off the moment.

When I woke up Tuesday afternoon, I noticed a guard at the door. He was standing with his back to me, but his khaki uniform broadcast his profession. On his hip I could see the handle of his revolver. "What's he there for?" I asked Bobby, my voice stronger now.

"Everybody wants to talk to you, honey. He's there to keep them away," my husband said. "When you keeled over in the coffee shop, the press was just across the street. They ran over when they heard the sirens and recognized you."

"The woman with the unforgettable eyes," I whispered, waves of sadness sweeping over me. "Why did Scott Wellen do it? Have you talked to him yet? Why'd he make my grief public before it was even private? What kind of a person is he?"

Bobby touched my lips. "Katie, you can't think about it. You need all your energy for yourself right now. Get stronger. Then we'll sort it all out. I'll help you, I promise. Can you just rest awhile? Please?"

He spoke so sweetly that I nodded my head. *I'll rest for awhile, dear Bobby, just for you. I'll rest just for you.*

"Close your eyes now, and I'll tell you a bedtime story." He moved his fingers to my eyes, gently closing my eyelids. "I'll tell you what I did yesterday after you left the office. And you try to go to sleep while I'm talking."

He pulled his chair closer to my bed, and spoke to me just above a whisper. "Ready?" I smiled and nodded, so he began. "After you left, I felt so alone I didn't know what to do. So I asked Kevin to take over for me and I went to the meadow."

"My meadow."

"Shhhh. Yes, your meadow. I sat on the rock where I found you last time. And I said to myself, 'Katie says there are words in the air. Maybe I can hear them if I listen with all my heart.' So I listened harder than I've ever listened before. Then I heard a story from a long time ago. One I hadn't thought of in years, maybe since I was 10.

"It's a story about a man and a butterfly. The butterfly, the only one of its kind in the whole universe, is so beautiful it makes the man happy just to look at it. And the man walks around all day with the butterfly on his shoulder.

"One day his neighbor says, 'That butterfly will get away from you if you don't grab him quick. You'd better catch him and hold him tight or you'll lose him.'

"So the man reaches up and grasps the butterfly in his hand, closing his palm on it tighter and tighter as the butterfly struggles to get away. Finally, the butterfly is quiet and the man dares to peek into his hand to look at his beautiful butterfly.

"But the butterfly isn't beautiful anymore. Its wings are folded, its body flattened, its life almost gone. So the man quickly puts the butterfly back on his shoulder, begging it to live and be beautiful again.

"Well, the butterfly does live. The man has taken it out of his fist in time. And when the butterfly recovers, they go walking together again. When the neighbor sees them, he calls out the same advice. 'That butterfly will get away from you if you don't grab him quick. You'd better catch him and hold him tight or you'll lose him.'

"But the man simply shakes his head and says, 'The truth, good neighbor, is that this beautiful butterfly is mine only as long as it's free.'"

Bobby's story echoed within me as I slept that evening, widening the boundaries I'd built around my inner self. And in my dreams that night, I was glad to be Bobby's wife.

24

obby Jay, you're crumpled!" He was still sitting
next to me when I woke again, his blonde hair
tangled, dark circles under his blue eyes. "You
look like you should be in this bed instead of me."

Bobby smiled, glad I was awake but unable to hide
his weariness.

"What time is it? How long have you been sitting
there?" I demanded.

"It's ten o'clock Wednesday morning. But I'm fine.
Just fine." He sat up straight, brushing his beard with
his palms and straightening his flannel shirt.

"You've been sitting there for two whole days?" I
asked.

"Not quite two days."

"Bobby Jay, you need to go home and sleep. Can't
someone else take your place?"

"You're in ICU, honey," he said hesitantly. "Only
your husband and parents are allowed in here with
you."

"Then get on the phone and call my mother," I
joked.

"Well . . . I suppose I could do that," he said.

"What?"

"Katie, you're not supposed to get excited," he took my hands in his, "but your mother is already here."

"You're kidding!" I sat upright. "Where?"

"Up the mountain with the girls." Bobby watched me cautiously.

"You're kidding!"

"Katie, please relax. Why would I kid you at a time like this?" He urged me back against the pillows. My heart fluttered rapidly, frightening me for a moment. "Call and tell her to come," I murmured as the feeling left me. "Then go on home for some rest."

"Are you sure? You won't be afraid to wait without me?"

"I won't be afraid." I could feel my mother's presence already. I wouldn't be afraid. I had never been afraid when she was with me. Then I remembered something else. "Carol's coming this afternoon," I told him. "Can you ask Karen to meet her at the airport so you can sleep? The girls could go along. They'd love it."

Bobby swallowed a smile. I knew he was trying desperately not to excite me, but his eyes were full of secrets he wanted to share. "She's already here too," he said matter-of-factly.

"Who else is here? Come on. I can see it in your eyes. Who else is here?"

"Meggie."

"Meggie!" There was still someone else in his look. "And who else?"

"Isn't that enough?"

"Bobby, who else?"

"The three musketeers together again," he teased. "Mayda flew in this morning. Carol went to pick her up."

"No wonder you looked like that," I said, overwhelmed at the thought of the three of us together again.

Bobby bent over and kissed me. "Go back to sleep now," he said. "If you're sure it's OK, I'll call your mother and then go get some shut-eye."

I nodded, requested a second kiss, and closed my eyes. *How come people in hospitals sleep so much,* I thought drowsily as I faded off again.

How come I feel so safe around you?" My mother was in the kitchen baking a cake for Karl's birthday. I was munching cookies at the table, gleeful at the prospect of a whole weekend without homework. It was my favorite time of day, coming home from school and finding her wherever she was. Then we'd talk—it didn't matter about what, it only mattered that I was with her, basking in her love.

"Children are supposed to feel safe with their parents," my mother observed as she cracked the eggs into the stainless steel mixing bowl. They landed inside with a plop.

"It's not an ordinary safeness. It's safeness like nothing in the world can possibly hurt me if you're near me. I don't feel that way around Daddy."

"Well, we all have our gifts," she said thoughtfully, measuring in the flour. "Sometimes I've thought my gift is acceptance, although at other times I've been certain it isn't. But maybe you feel that way with me because I accept you just as you are, because I never ask you to prove anything to me."

It was a funny answer, one I hadn't expected, but it made sense as I contemplated it to the rhythm of the oatmeal and raisin crunching in my mouth. My mother was unique among the adults I knew. I wasn't the only one who felt it. When she substitute taught at Hope Academy, other students remarked on it too. Maybe that was what they felt—her unqualified acceptance.

And maybe that was safety, never having to perform for love.

"Who makes you feel that way, safe like that?" I asked impulsively, certain it wasn't my father and wondering who it could be then. Was there anyone who gave my mother the same blessing she bestowed on me?

"All people fail you sooner or later, Katie," she said, wiping her hands on her apron and coming to join me at the table. "I will fail you some time."

"No you won't," I said emphatically.

"Yes, I will. All people will fail you sometime or other. Not because they want to, but because they're human. I wouldn't be a good mother if I didn't tell you that. There's only one direction we can look for complete safety, unfailing security. It's not out to other people, but up to God.

"That's one of the main lessons you must learn before you can truly grow up. But unfortunately, you can't learn it from someone else, not even from me. It's a truth that must be lived into your life through experience, usually difficult experience."

She took a cookie, hugged me, and went back to her baking. "The only place I find the kind of safety you're talking about is with the Lord. And I'm afraid, my darling, that the time will come when you'll find it necessary to transfer that fierce loyalty of yours from me to Him."

Her soft hands stroked my forehead. They were the same strong, loving hands that had dried my tears and held me tight for so many years. I didn't have to open my eyes to know she was there. Her touch was so beloved and familiar no one in the world could have duplicated it.

"Hi, Mommy."

"Katie."

And then I cried all the tears that hadn't come since I'd realized deep down inside, that Daryl was gone. All the anguish I hadn't been able to face without her. She had loved him. She had been a mother to him. She had listened to him, and prayed for him, and accepted him along with the rest of her brood.

I could cry with her because we would cry together. And as I sobbed in her arms, the strength of my defenses became clear to me. I had known from the beginning that Daryl had painted the portrait of me in *People* magazine. And I had known he would never relinquish me to another man's fantasies. I had known Daryl was dead.

When we finally talked, it wasn't about Daryl or about what had happened to me. It was about Daddy and Karl, Big John, Lita, and Little John, about Meggie, Carol, and Mayda, and about her granddaughters, Susie, Janie, and Missy. Comfortable, homey talk.

I wanted to get well. I wanted to hold my daughters in my arms and tell them how much I loved them. I wanted to be better and stronger than I'd ever been before. I wanted to be as good a mother to them as my mother was to me.

"The doctor says he might move you out of ICU tonight," my mother said, after she ran out of anecdotes. "Then if you're strong enough, you can have visitors."

"I'll be strong enough," I promised. "I'm going to get well as fast as I can. I just want to go home and be with all my favorite people."

25

D r. Hammel, our family physician, was a hairy giant of a man that made even Bobby look small. "God made me this way so my patients will know who's boss," he said as he poked and peeked and listened. "This room is for sick people, little girl. I don't know what you're doing here."

It was Wednesday evening, and Bobby was back. "I think you've brought your wife here under false pretenses, sir," Dr. Hammel said, glaring at him severely.

Bobby feigned terror of the man who had supervised his entrance into the world. "Where should she be then, sir?" he asked him.

"Back home where she belongs," Dr. Hammel answered, "but as long as she's here, we'll humor her in a private room for a few days." He picked up my chart and wrote, hiding his pleasure at my progress behind it.

Dr. Hammel was devoted to the Carson clan, winding his way up the mountain if house calls were necessary. Father and Mother Carson's confidence in him as a young doctor struggling to establish a practice had been repayed time and again as he cared for their bountiful family.

"He's been sleeping in the doctor's lounge since they brought you in," Bobby whispered as two orderlies wheeled me out of ICU. "The old duffer just doesn't know how to say he cares."

He doesn't have to, I thought. *He's always there. And that's enough.*

In my new room, my mother and my husband fussed over me and praised me until the night nurse sent them home. "No more all night vigils," she said firmly. "In this part of the hospital, we have visiting hours.

"The two of you may be here any time between nine in the morning and nine at night. Visiting hours for friends are two to four in the afternoon and seven to nine at night. But only two people in the room at a time. And please remind visitors that Katie is here to rest. This is a hospital, not a hotel."

"Tell Carol to come tomorrow afternoon," I told Bobby as he kissed me good night. "I'm still worried about her."

"She's fine," he reassured me. "You'll see."

Shortly after my mother and Bobby left, Dr. Hammel's great frame filled the doorway. "May I come in?" he asked politely.

"You're the doctor." I smiled, thinking how much I liked this man of few words.

"I brought you a sleeping pill." He placed a white container on the table next to my bed. "But before you take it, I want to talk to you." Then he sat down so his head was level with mine, cleared his throat, and squirmed.

Finally he dove into it. "I'll be straight with you, Katie. I asked Bobby not to bring up the shock that precipitated the heart attack until you were out of ICU.

It was important for you to remain calm. Now it's important for you to deal with your friend's death. The best way for you to get well is to face your grief. Do you understand what I'm saying?"

"Yes," I said. "You're saying I won't get well if I don't face Daryl's death."

Dr. Hammel nodded. "I'm also saying you won't get well if you don't let go." He stood up, turning on his gruff charm, relief visible on his face. "Those are orders," he said as he marched out of the room.

My mother came at nine the next morning, saying Bobby had business to attend to until late afternoon. He called me at noon to apologize, but I said it was wonderful to watch life return to normal.

Carol knocked on the door at precisely two o'clock. She looked just the same. The same strong, intelligent handsomeness. The same tailored, open carriage. She sparkled as she walked over to me. "I thought you were tired, burned out, needing R 'n R," I said as we embraced.

"That was last week. So much can happen in a week." She laughed, then backed away cautiously, holding me at arm's length and searching my face. "Are you going to be all right?"

"Yes, I am," I said with certainty.

Carol greeted my mother fondly, not having seen her since high school. My mother remarked on how much we'd grown, making all the usual motherly observations upon surveying old charges. Then she excused herself, leaving us alone to talk.

"I want to hear about you," I told Carol. "I'm sure you know all about me from Bobby. Now I want to know what's been going on with you. Something was wrong, I know it."

"You're right." Carol took the seat of honor next to my bed. "Something was wrong."

"It wasn't just burnout."

"It wasn't just burnout." She laughed at me fondly. "Are you sure you want to hear this? If I start at the beginning, I'll have to go through right to the end."

"Start at the beginning and go right through to the end," I commanded.

"Well, it began with Mark Whittacker." Carol looked past me through the window blinds to the afternoon sunshine beyond. "Mark heads up—I should say headed up, it still sounds strange—our task force."

She went on to tell me a story with enough twists and turns, intrigue and subterfuge to fill a spy novel. The short of it was that Mark had been on the take, and Carol had gradually discovered it, substantiated it, and brought charges against him. The long of it was that she had been in love with him.

"When I began to suspect that Mark was taking bribes, I wanted to know more so I could prove to myself that he wasn't," she said when she finished the story. "Then I had to find out more because I had to know how bad it was. Finally, I had to discover it all, to take it to the end because it was the only way to resolve it."

She was quiet. I waited for her to continue, but when she didn't, I asked, "What was in Wichita? Kansas isn't on the way to California from Colorado."

"You noticed!" She seemed delighted that I'd brought it up. "There's a man in Kansas. No, not that kind of man," she added noticing the look on my face. "This is an elderly man, a friend of my grandmother's. I don't have words to describe him to you." She held her hands up in a helpless gesture. "He's . . . "

"Well, what did he do to you?" I interrupted.

"He didn't *do* anything. He just was. And I spent two days with him just being. I wouldn't have believed I could be ready to rush out here, to handle—everything.

I was so low, so very low. But I spent two days in God's presence, or at least in the presence of someone who reflects Him more accurately than anyone I've known before. And I was restored. More than restored. It's as if I've been reborn."

She grasped my bed rail. "Katie, it was like visiting Mary and Joseph in the stable, and meeting the Christ Child, so unexpected, so unassuming, so . . . " She ran out of words, but something passed between us, something sweet and satisfying.

"I'm so glad." I reached out to hug her, blessing the wonderfulness of her experience although I didn't understand it. "I'm so glad."

Meggie and Mayda energized the evening visiting hours, blasting in like two stars from heaven. "You look wonderful! Marvelous!" they assured me, and proceeded to entertain me with tales from their far-flung worlds, compressing the two hours into what felt like a few short minutes.

They both seemed so young to me as I watched them cavort around the room, illustrating whatever nonsense they were describing—Meggie because she was still young, Mayda because she had never grown up. I loved them for being so simple, so transparent, so reachable.

Shortly before nine, there was a hurried conference in the bathroom. Meggie rushed out to borrow a pillow, explaining it was for a skit, a "bedtime drama." Then she took my suitcase from the closet and disappeared back into the bathroom saying, "Don't worry, Big Sister. The costuming will only take a minute. This will be folk art. Very *in*, you know."

Two minutes later, Meggie was back, holding the suitcase and rushing about the room in a panic. "Doctor! Doctor! This woman needs a doctor. Doctor! Why isn't there ever a doctor when you need one?" Then she hissed under her breath, "Ask me what's wrong, who needs a doctor, and why?"

"What's wrong?" I asked obediently. "Who needs a doctor? And why?"

"This woman!" Meggie flung open the bathroom door. "And this is why!" Mayda waddled out.

"You're kidding!" I stared at the pillow under Mayda's dress in astonishment. "After all these years? You're not kidding! Does Carlos know? Did you plan it?"

Mayda nodded, glowing all over.

"Oh, May, I'm so happy for you! I'm going to be an auntie. Oh, Mayda!" I held out my arms. *So even Mayda's changing,* I thought as we hugged around the pillow. *Mayda and Carlos who thought they were enough for each other for all time. They're changing too.*

26

I was awake when Bobby arrived Friday morning.
"Hi, handsome!" It felt good to greet someone first
for a change.

"How's my favorite patient?" He whipped a bouquet
of daisies from behind his back and kissed me lightly
on the nose.

"Impatient to get out of here."

"That's my favorite wife."

"Are there more?" I wiggled my nose, trying to itch
where he'd kissed me. "You gave me an itch."

"May I?" He scratched it with his forefinger.
"Better?"

"Yeah." I motioned to the chair. "Now that you've
flattered me and kissed my nose—all necessary
preliminaries—it's time to talk."

"Talk time, children." Bobby smiled inanely, on the
verge of his Mr. Rogers routine.

"I'm serious, honey."

"I know. I guess I was just hoping to see you smile a
little more before . . . " He slouched back. "Tell me."

"Tell me" had started when we were going together.
It meant "it's your turn to say what's on your mind. I'll

listen until you're finished." Slouching was his characteristic pose for "tell me" times.

"So much has happened to me in the past week . . . " I hesitated. I wanted to be calm, logical. I needed to organize my emotions, to sort them out efficiently so they wouldn't overwhelm me.

"I guess there's a lot of things I don't know yet. I don't even remember everything Mr. Atwater told me. I remember the video, and that's about all. Did you watch the video? Did Mr. Atwater give it to you?"

Bobby nodded. "Will it help if I tell you what I know?" he asked.

"Would you, please?"

"Scott Wellen left a message on the recorder. I found it when I got back from the meadow, and returned his call. I've also talked to Mr. Atwater, seen the death certificate, and the video. The will can't be read until you're able—"

"There was something . . . " I interrupted.

Bobby waited, but the vague memory eluded me and I motioned for him to continue. "You know Daryl was hunting wild boar in the interior of Kalimantan. Unfortunately, the postmarks on the cards you received were misleading. I assume he sent them out to the coast, and they were mailed inadvertently after his death."

"Was it a wild boar?" I whispered.

Bobby reached for my hand. "He broke his neck diving off a cliff, Katie. He lived for three days, though most of that time he was delirious. He only gained consciousness shortly before the end. By then, a missionary had been brought to him."

"A missionary?"

Bobby squeezed my hand. "The time of death was 3:49 in the afternoon, September twenty-second," he went on. "The missionary buried him, and then cabled

Scott Wellen advising him of the accident.

"Daryl had given Scott instructions in the event of his death, asking him to contact Atwater and Klein, and wait for you to get in touch with him. That's why he didn't call you directly."

"September twenty-second at 3:49 in the afternoon? What day of the week was that?" I asked in a small voice.

"It was a Tuesday their time, Katie. But it was late Monday evening our time."

"We were asleep," I whispered. "We were asleep when Daryl died."

"Yes, Katie." Bobby said sorrowfully. "We were asleep."

"And he died with a missionary beside him." I felt very tired. "Why did Scott Wellen wait so long to call the lawyers?" I asked, grasping for some other emotion to steady myself. "Just so he could get the article in *People* first? Didn't he realize what it would lead to?" I pointed toward the uniform outside the door.

"I think he did, honey. I don't think you're going to like Scott Wellen very much. I'll handle him for you if you want me to." I could hear the anger in Bobby's voice. "His business is to sell books. This kind of publicity sells books. He waited to contact Atwater and Klein until he knew the magazine had gone to press."

"Am I a very rich woman?"

"Rich and famous in one stroke. How's that?" Bobby grinned for the first time since he had said "tell me." "Daryl left you everything. Scott told me it's in the millions. Apparently, under his three pseudonyms, your high school friend was one of the most successful writers in the world."

"He must have just dashed them off," I said, bewildered at the thought.

"Scott says Daryl could write a book faster than

most folks can read one. He'd write a novel in four days, toss it at his agent, and rush off. He never rewrote or reread any of them. He could have been a great writer, Katie, if he had wanted to. Instead, he was just successful."

"Great writers leave something behind," I whispered, recognizing Daryl's logic. I rested back on the pillows and closed my eyes, speaking not just to Bobby but to myself as well. "I can get crazy sometimes thinking about him, about his life."

I saw Daryl vividly in my mind, standing on the sandy beach, his hair blowing in the breeze. "But that's not new for me. It's something I've fought ever since I met him—thinking that if I could only do this or be that, it would help him.

"I can think that if I'd married him, he wouldn't be dead now. But I know it's not true. You know, sometimes before I married you, I used to let myself pretend that Daryl and I were 'going together,' that we were romantically involved. I was always amazed at what happened to me inside.

"The distance that allowed our friendship to be was gone and in its place was a possessiveness, a desperate need for him to change. I don't know how we always knew we would ruin each other if we tried to be more than friends. It was a precocious understanding. But then nothing about our friendship was ordinary.

"Still, I don't understand exactly how I was tied to him, how I'm still tied. It's so hard, Bobby, to believe he's really dead. There's no body to bury."

Bobby moved to the edge of the bed and took me into his arms. "Maybe you won't really know Daryl's gone until Christmas when he doesn't come home, Katie," he said.

I buried myself in his embrace. Somewhere in the background voices chattered and buzzers rang, but I knew they weren't for me. *Daryl's dead,* I told myself over and over, his vibrant image from the video tape so incredibly alive in my mind. *He's dead and you'll never see him again. Not in life or in death.*

This body is nothing." Daryl stood on the hill overlooking Hope Academy, his tall, lean body braced against the wind. It didn't look like nothing to me. "You're supposed to believe that, Eyes. This body is corruptible, remember?"

"Still, letting someone toss you into a furnace like a dead animal at the pound . . . " I shuddered.

"I won't feel a thing." Daryl tossed back his head and laughed, so alive I couldn't picture him dead. "I'm leaving nothing behind. Not even ashes. I'm having them scattered across the ocean.

"When I die, I want you to take my ashes, rent a helicopter, and fly out over the blue expanse." He stretched his arms toward Manila Bay like a preacher at a hell fire and brimstone tent revival. "Yes, Sister Katherine, it is my desire, I say, my fervent wish, for you to take the silver vial containing the remains of my earthly body.

"I say, take those remains, find a mechanical bird. I say, find a bird to soar through the sky like a winged cherubim." His voice rose and fell in a melodic cadence. "And when you have reached the pinnacle of the celestial firmament, I say Sister Katherine, take those remains and scatter them across the blue, oh so blue, expanse of the wide open ocean.

"And so I will live forever only in your heart." He folded his hands over his chest.

"Well, if that's really what you want, you'd better get rich before you die and leave me a lot of money because helicopters cost a bundle," I griped, not at all amused with his little production.

Daryl curled his lip and clicked his tongue. "So serious, Sister Katherine, for one so young. How will you ever learn to soar like an eagle?"

"You be an eagle. I'll settle for being a duck. They never get too far off the ground, but when they fall, it isn't fatal."

27

Bobby stayed until late that afternoon. He must have put a hold on other visitors because no one else came. I was grateful. When he left, shortly before the supper hour, I felt lonelier than I'd ever felt before in my life. I wanted to call to him, to beg him not to leave, but I didn't. Somehow I knew it was a loneliness I'd been avoiding far too long, a loneliness no one else could push back for me.

I clicked on the remote to the television, needing the comfort of voices but not wanting to watch. Then I stared at the institutional clock on the wall and followed the second hand on its weary race around the face.

At exactly six o'clock, a speckle-haired volunteer in a pink coat brought my dinner. She set the tray on the table beside me, lifted the cover from the plate, made a face, and swung the table over me. "This is a disgrace," she whispered. "The salad has green onions."

"You don't like onions?" I inquired politely.

"They don't like me," she announced. Then she sat down uninvited in the chair Bobby had vacated only 10 minutes before. "If I rested here, I wouldn't bother you. We wouldn't have to talk or anything. The bunkles on my feet are paining me right now."

"Bunkles?" I stared at her curiously. *Sixty, sixty-five,* I thought, memorizing her so I'd have something new to tell my visitors the next day. *More white than gray. Her glasses are kind of twisted or something. They don't sit right. It makes her look sort of surprised. There's something interesting about her, something unusual. She's timid, and yet sure of herself. The lines on her face are all happy lines.*

"Bunkles. They're bunions. Willie, my husband, called them bunkles because my name is Mrs. Carbunkle. I loved my husband, bless his soul. Otherwise I wouldn't have traded Foster for Carbunkle. My maiden name was Foster. Can you imagine?

"This is such a happy time for me." She seemed to twinkle all over. "My daughter, Trina, is having a baby. Can you believe she already knows it's a boy? I have nine other grandchildren, but I'm going to actually see this one be born!

"Can you imagine? I had five children of my own and I wasn't awake for any of them. Five children and nine grandchildren, and I've never watched a baby being born. Trina's having my grandson at a birthing center. As soon as she goes into labor, I'm taking the bus to Anaheim. I didn't want to leave my work here until the last minute because I'll be staying with her to help her for at least a month.

"There, I've talked your ear off when I said I would be quiet, and you haven't eaten a thing." She wrinkled her nose again at the thought of my food.

"I don't mind. It's been interesting." I picked up my spoon to stir my soup. "You can sit there awhile longer if you want to."

Mrs. Carbunkle reached into her pocket. "That's very kind," she said. "I'd like a moment to study my Scripture."

"Oh, do you memorize a different Scripture verse each day? I have an aunt who does that."

She hesitated. "Memorize a Scripture verse each day? I hadn't thought of that. It seems rather hasty. I usually take all year on one."

"All year? You must pick very long ones."

She hesitated again. "I guess that depends on whose measurement you use," she said mysteriously. "All I know is that I've been soaking in this one since January, and soon the year will be up. I'll miss it. But I always feel that way when the year is over, and I have to move on to a new one."

She unfolded a small piece of paper and began to study it. Thinking it impolite to intrude upon her devotional, I tried to eat my meat loaf but I soon found myself asking, "Would you mind reading it to me?" I felt I had to find out what was on that dog-eared slip of paper, what portion of the Bible could possibly take a year to "soak in."

"Oh, that would be *wonderful!*" Mrs. Carbunkle beamed as if the possibility hadn't occurred to her. "That would be wonderful." She adjusted her glasses, cleared her throat, and began.

"Before the dawn-wind rises, before the shadows flee, I will go to the mountain of myrrh, to the hill of frankincense. For me the reward of virtue is to see your face, and, on waking, to gaze my fill on your likeness."

She looked at the paper while she spoke, but I knew she was quoting, loving every syllable of every word. We were quiet for a short time that seemed very long, then she apologized, "I'm afraid I cheated just a little bit. I've put two Scriptures together. One from the Song of Songs and one from the Psalms."

She lowered her voice to a conspiratorial whisper and leaned forward to confide in me. "It's from *The Jerusalem Bible.* I wouldn't say this to just anyone, but you'll understand. *The Jerusalem Bible* has a special melody to it. It's so much more modern than the King James. My husband would pass on at the thought, if he hadn't already." She glanced about the room as if searching for ghosts. "He was something of a fuddy-duddy, you know."

Just then a nurse stuck her head into the room. "Mrs. Carbunkle?"

"I'll be right there, dear," my new friend said cheerfully. "Would you like this?" she asked as she stood up. "I can make another for myself when I get home."

I took the torn paper eagerly. "Yes, I would."

"How lovely." She looked as if I'd given her a gift. "How lovely to pass it on."

I read it over and over after she left, pushing aside my dinner tray and spreading the paper out in front of me, smoothing its creases against the metal. It was like a coded message. Or I was like a dyslexic, seeing all the symbols but unable to translate them. The words were so beautiful, and yet all I could understand was that they were somehow terribly important.

Sometime later, Mrs. Carbunkle returned for my tray. When she saw I was still reading, she clapped in delight. "Enjoy the beauty of it," she said as she left. "The understanding comes as you enjoy the beauty. You must go to the mountain, before the dawn-wind rises, if you wish to see His face. Being there, being ready for Him, is all that really matters." And then she was gone again without saying good-bye.

My mother came that evening. I was still pondering Mrs. Carbunkle's words, still had the paper before me, when she arrived. Instead of showing it to her, I shoved it quickly under the covers. It was too new to me. I needed more time.

Then something I had forgotten pushed at my brain, something I'd almost remembered when I was talking to Bobby. My mother greeted me, but I held up my hand. "Just a minute," I whispered. "I'm trying to remember something."

Gradually, it came back. "Mr. Atwater gave me a letter." I motioned excitedly for my purse. "He said Scott Wellen had passed it on to him. It's from the missionary who was with Daryl. It's for me." My mother found my bag and handed it to me, bewilderment on her face.

It was there in the side pocket. "Here it is!" My hand shook as I pulled it out. On the outside of the brown envelope it said, "Mr. Wellen, please pass this on to someone named Katie. Apparently, she is a close friend of Mr. Coombs. A package of Mr. Coombs' personal effects follows." The envelope was sealed.

"Would you like me to read it to you?" my mother asked.

I handed her the envelope, my hands still shaking, and leaned back on the pillows to listen.

Dear Katie,
I am writing to you because I believe Daryl Coombs wanted to leave you a message. When I reached him, he had been unconscious for almost 36 hours. His neck was broken and he had no movement below the shoulders.

"I stayed beside him, making him as comfortable as I could, praying for him constantly. Your friend had been in a troubled delirium, but after the second day, he grew peaceful. He floated in and out of consciousness the day he died. He only spoke once. Minutes before he died, he opened his eyes and whispered, 'Tell Katie I won't be as enough . . . '

"I'm sorry it wasn't more. Perhaps you will know what was on his mind. He seemed content with what he had said, not struggling to complete the sentence, and passed away quite peacefully.

"I am enclosing my address in case you want to write to me or come to visit his grave. I'm also sending a small box of his personal effects to Mr. Wellen. My deepest sympathies.

Arthur S. Webster."

"I won't be as enough?" My mother studied me questioningly.

I don't believe a good God is behind all the pain in this world. But if the Bible turns out to be true and I stand at the judgment, I'm not going to be ass enough to defend my opinion. I'll just bow down and confess I was wrong. I'll ask God to forgive me. If He is a good God, he won't toss a repentant sinner into hell. And if He's a bad God, heaven will be hell just like earth is so the whole thing will be academic.

I gripped the covers, pouring out a lifetime of resistance through my fingertips. There was nothing more I could do. Daryl was gone, gone to prove the truth of his words.

And then I knew—suddenly like a Polaroid photograph swiftly materializes where seconds before there was no image—that Daryl had been a wall for me, both protecting and preventing me from faith. Because he couldn't believe, neither could I, although I had lacked his courage. My unbelief had been passive, hidden even to myself.

"For a long time, I've had this feeling of being a coward." I turned toward my mother, my voice hoarse and low. "Daryl acted out his unbelief. I think I just hid mine. But if it's true, what reason do I have? Daryl had reasons—he lost his mother. His life was awful. But why should I doubt God? I've never known anything but love."

My mother moved her lips silently. When she spoke, she said, "Perhaps you've confused the Creator with the created, Katie. You've been raised in the church, and you've seen so much hypocrisy. I think Daryl was the first person you perceived as completely real, truly honest. And yet everyone else rejected him.

"Perhaps you felt deep inside that God rejected him too. You are so loyal, honey. Perhaps deep inside you couldn't believe in a God you thought had rejected a boy who needed Him so much. You didn't realize God was loving him through you."

Tears crept down her cheeks. "Instead of seeing Christ, Katie, you saw Christians. Unfortunately, there can be a vast difference between the two."

28

Mrs. Carbunkle was out of uniform when she placed my breakfast tray on the table Saturday morning. "I'm not really on duty, dear," she confided in a whisper, her salt and pepper hair askew, and her glasses balanced precariously on her nose.

"I just got the call. Trina's in the hospital. I'm on my way to the bus station now. It's so exciting! I'm actually going to see my own grandson be born. I want you to pray for me, little girl. I wouldn't want to faint or anything."

"I will. I certainly will," I assured her as she uncovered the hot dish, made a face at the oatmeal, and swung the table over me. "Shouldn't you be going?" I asked. "It's so sweet of you to come, but you didn't have to. I'm doing fine."

"Oh, yes. I'd better be going." She backed away from the bed and stood, hands behind her back, waiting for something.

I wondered if she wanted me to taste my food before she left, so I picked up the spoon and dipped it into the bowl. "It's fine. Not too lumpy," I said, hoping that would satisfy her. The oatmeal was soupy and I wanted to avoid it.

Mrs. Carbunkle patted her hair and adjusted her glasses, still waiting.

"You look wonderful. Thank you so much for coming." I tried a farewell again, covering all the niceties I could think of. "Have a pleasant trip."

She clasped her hands in front of her this time, still waiting.

"Is there something you'd like to tell me before you go, Mrs. Carbunkle?" I asked, guessing correctly this time.

"Well, yes there is." She bit her bottom lip nervously. "It's just a little something I wrote a long time ago. I was about your age. I'm not a writer, you know, but this just came to me." She seemed to gain confidence now that I knew the real reason for her visit.

"I'm going to be late if I don't hurry. I really must run." She reached into her big pocket, took out several folded sheets of paper, and placed them on the table. "It's just a little story. I haven't shown it to anyone.

"But yesterday when we were talking, you reminded me so much of myself. I just thought . . . well, it helped me so much, I just thought it might help you too, dear."

And then she left, jabbering to herself excitedly about the adventure ahead of her. I picked up the sheets of paper and began to read, my breakfast growing cold in front of me, touched only by the tears that fell as I read.

THE MINNOW CREEK

He was sitting beside the creek where I went every day to watch the minnows chasing each other over the rocks and under the slime. I think I had sensed his presence before. I must have. The creek with the minnows and the rocks was the most peaceful place I had ever known.

I must have sensed his presence there before, because when I saw him, I knew he was the reason I had first come and he was the reason I came back day after day, year after year. I knew I had never seen him before, and yet he was the most familiar person I had ever met. I felt no fear and so I sat down on the rocks beside him.

"Hello," I said. "You belong here, don't you?"

He looked at me and smiled gently. "Yes, I do."

"Thank you for sharing your brook with me."

He smiled again. "You're welcome. The best part of my day has been sharing it with you."

I looked at the minnows darting under and over the slime and then looked back at him. "Why haven't I seen you before? I come here often. Every day, in fact."

"You've been so busy collecting. You do have quite a collection. I have called to you before, but you've been so intent on your work, I guess you didn't hear me. I've been sitting here for years—from the beginning in fact. I've enjoyed your visits, watching you. You certainly do put your heart and soul into your collection. Do you have it with you? May I see what you've been putting yourself into with such intensity all these years?"

I had it with me. I glanced down at my rock collection, clutched tightly in my hand. It was wrapped in a red bandana and was quite heavy by now. He was right. Years of hard work and much of my best thought had gone into making my collection. I looked up at him and tightened my grip on my bandana.

"You've been watching me, so you've seen how much work I have put into this. You must have noticed that only the best rocks have become part of my collection. Each one is special and the product of a long search. No rock is in my collection by chance. You might think that after so many years of collecting I would have hundreds of rocks, but I don't. Each one is so special and so important that I've spent up to a year searching for just one."

"Yes, I've seen how you go about it. You've been quite careful and selective. May I see your collection?" His eyes were on my red bandana and I clutched it tighter.

"It's not as if I came upon them by chance," I explained. "Each one was in my mind. I created each one in my mind and then went out to find it. I didn't see it and then think of it. I thought of it, and then went out to find it. That has been my method. And that's why my collection is so precious and why it has taken so much time."

We sat next to each other and watched the minnows. I didn't look at him, and for awhile I tried to pretend he wasn't there. But the peace was still there, and I knew now that it came from him—not from the creek or the minnows or the rocks. I knew he had been there all along and had watched my whole collection take shape—from the first beautiful blue rock to the twenty-eighth one, the gold one with the silver specks.

He turned to me again. "May I see your collection?"

I looked at him, and was comforted by the knowledge that he had been there all along. "You know how much my collection means to me. It's taken me my whole life. I'm afraid it might not seem like much to you, wrapped in a red bandana and all. It might not seem very precious."

He looked back at me and smiled with his eyes. It was a deep, warming smile that went way inside me, and I relaxed my grip on my bandana.

"I know how much it means to you," he said softly. "You've worked your whole life to collect it. I value it too. Much of who you are is in your collection. I value you."

I knelt down on the sand beside where he sat and

spread the bandana out in front of him. I arranged the rocks as I always did, slowly and carefully, stopping to remember the day I found each one. Each was special and yet, some more so than others. I always took a little longer to arrange the most special ones.

When each was in place, I sat back on the sand and looked up for his reaction. I was surprised to find he hadn't turned to my collection. He was still looking at me, "See, here it is," I said, pointing to it. "I don't want to sound proud, but I do believe it's perfect."

He looked at the rocks arranged so carefully on the red bandana in four rows of seven each. The sun gleamed and glinted off each one. A speck of dust settled on the third from the right in the fourth row, and I reached down to wipe it off with the special yellow cloth I carried for that purpose. When I looked up at him again, his eyes were back on me.

He smiled again, this time not just with his eyes, but with his whole body. It was a big, joyful smile that made me think I'd never seen the sun before. "May I have one of your rocks?" He reached out his hand.

I fell back. "What?"

He smiled the same joyful sun-filled smile. "May I have one of your rocks?"

I looked down at my collection. Which one could I part with? I went down the rows, counting each one, looking to see if there was one I could part with, one my collection would be intact without. I shook my head. "I can't find any to give you," I said. "I'm sorry. There is none I can part with.

"You must understand. You've been here all along. You've seen my work. You must understand. Each rock is an integral part of my collection. I can't part with any. I am sorry." I gazed at the sand. I had been looking down at my collection as I spoke, and now I felt I couldn't bear to look up at him.

We sat quietly for a long time. He didn't speak. I knew he was looking at me. But I didn't look at him. I could hear the water running down the creek and feel the wind tugging softly at my hair. I dug my hands into the sand and it was warm. I sat looking at it for a very long time.

Then I remembered his smile and the way his eyes had warmed me way inside where I'd never been warm before. I thought of the joy—almost glee—with which he had asked for one of my rocks. I looked up at him, but my gaze fell back to the sand almost as soon as it caught his face.

I had not been prepared for what I saw. When I looked at him, I saw deepest love and deepest pain. I knew then that I had never seen love or pain before. How should I respond to this man from whom all peace and joy, love and pain seemed to radiate? How should I respond to the one who had been there from the beginning?

I reached down, picked up my jade, and put it in the hand that had remained outstretched. His hand closed on it slowly. Then with his fist, he gently lifted my chin until he was looking into my face. Pain and love were still there mixed together on his face, and I knew it was my pain he felt. "Thank you," he said softly. "May I have another rock?"

We sat there for days; perhaps it was weeks. I can't account for the time. One by one, I gave him the rocks from my collection. I watched it dwindle from 28 to none. I put each rock carefully into his outstretched hand, and he carefully closed his fingers over it. When he put out his hand to ask for another, the previous rock was gone. I didn't ask him where they went.

With some of the rocks, we sat in silence for days before I parted with them. With others, we talked long and deep. Sometimes I cried. He cried too, although his tears were for me and not for himself. Sometimes I reasoned and argued. He listened patiently, but never waivered from his original request. For some reason, I gave up numbers 17 and 26 without even being asked.

His response was always the same whether it had taken a long time or a short time. "Thank you." And the love and the pain on his face could not be separated.

When I had given him the last rock, I rolled up the red bandana and the yellow cloth and put them into his hand. These too disappeared. Then I reached out my hand and put it in his. "We have been in this garden a long time together, haven't we?" I asked.

Looking around, I noticed that it was indeed a garden. While we had been together, flowers and trees of every kind had grown up around us. Wildlife had made the garden their home, and none of them seemed to know fear. The creek had widened and become a stream so glad to be that it shouted for joy. The minnows in the creek had been joined by fish of all colors and sizes, uniting in an underwater dance of celebration.

I looked into the face of the one whose hand I held. "This is a celebration of *you*," I said.

His face broke out in that sun-filled joy I had come to know. "This is a celebration of *us*," He replied. "Since you don't need to spend your time collecting rocks anymore, you may spend your time here with me. We will spend all time here together celebrating US."

29

When Bobby arrived at 10, he brought a small box that obviously had traveled a long distance. "Scott Wellen sent it express," he explained as he handed me the brown wrapped package. "I thought you'd want it right away."

"Thank you."

He took a knife from his pocket, cut the ragged string, unwrapped the paper, and handed me a beige shoe box proclaiming some brand of Indonesian footwear. Inside was a legal sized yellow sheet listing the items of Daryl's clothing and equipment that remained with Mr. Webster.

"I will send the above with Grover Harris, a fellow missionary, who returns on furlough in January," it said at the bottom. "Enclosed are smaller items I thought would be appreciated sooner."

Inside some tissue paper were Daryl's wallet, watch, jade ring, and datebook. Beside them were three small white boxes—each containing a tiny jeweled princess ring. I handed these to Bobby.

"Daryl's extra 'special' Christmas presents for the girls. They're from Thailand. Each tiny jewel signifies a special blessing for the wearer," I explained, pointing to the delicate jewels encased in the silver cones.

"They're beautiful. The girls will love them." Bobby lifted the smallest one to the light. "And they're adjustable."

"Bobby?"

"Yes?"

"How will we tell them their Uncle Daryl is gone?"

"Together." He reached for my hand. "When you come home, we'll tell them together—maybe in the meadow."

"We should give them the rings then instead of at Christmas. They should have a symbol, something to hang on to."

"Katie?"

"Yes?"

"Our life is going to be different now. I don't know exactly how, but Fallstown doesn't seem so important anymore. You were right. There's a bigger world out there."

"Can I read you something?"

"Please."

I felt for the worn slip of paper under my pillow, smoothed it out against my knees, and read deliberately as if all creation waited upon my words.

"Before the dawn-wind rises, before the shadows flee, I will go to the mountain of myrrh, to the hill of frankincense. For me the reward of virtue is to see your face, and, on waking, to gaze my fill on your likeness."

"It's beautiful," Bobby whispered.

"Mrs. Carbunkle says we must go to the mountain, before the dawn-wind rises, if we wish to see His face. She says being there, being ready for Him, is all that really matters."

"Mrs. Carbunkle?"

I laughed. "I haven't told you about Mrs. Carbunkle

yet, have I? She's sort of a prophetess, I think, although she'd perish if she heard me say so. Do you understand what I just read?"

"No, not exactly."

"But you recognize its beauty. That's what's important. Mrs. Carbunkle says understanding comes as you enjoy the beauty."

We were quiet together, wondering at the Old Testament words. There was more to tell him—about Mrs. Carbunkle, about the minnow creek. But there would be time for that, and more. All I needed to know now was that he recognized the beauty and felt its power.

I put Daryl's things back in the shoebox, saving them for another time too. Someday I'd take them out and cry because he was gone. *I'll cry for me,* I thought as I handed the box to Bobby, *for my own loss. Daryl's off on another adventure. Maybe he's found the party that has no end.*

"Bobby?" I reached for his hand.

"Yeah?" He held my fingertips to his lips.

"What will we do with the money?"

He laughed. "Well, we won't spend it all in one place," he said, repeating his father's favorite admonition when we had a few extra dollars. "We won't spend it all in one place."